PRAISE FOR *MOMS LIKE US*

"*Moms Like Us* is a fun and juicy page-turner about the extreme and often criminal lengths some parents will go."

—Amy Poehler, actress, producer, and author of *Yes Please*

"It's a thin line between mental load and murder for these Los Angeles moms with the best intentions who will do anything to protect their children and their reputations. *Moms Like Us* is a hysterical, satirical, sexy novel you won't be able to put down!"

—Melissa de la Cruz, *New York Times* bestselling author

"Seriously hilarious and embarrassingly relatable, *Moms Like Us* explores the deliciously dark lengths mothers will go in the name of self-preservation on the bumpy road toward ensuring their children thrive."

—Erica Katz, author of the novels *The Boys' Club* and *Fake*

MOMS LIKE US

MOMS LIKE US

a novel

Jordan Roter

Little
a

Text copyright © 2025 by Jordan Roter
All rights reserved.

No part of this book may be reproduced, or stored in a retrieval system, or transmitted in any form or by any means, electronic, mechanical, photocopying, recording, or otherwise, without express written permission of the publisher.

Published by Little A, New York

www.apub.com

Amazon, the Amazon logo, and Little A are trademarks of Amazon.com, Inc., or its affiliates.

EU product safety contact:
Amazon Media EU S. à r.l.
38, avenue John F. Kennedy, L-1855 Luxembourg
amazonpublishing-gpsr@amazon.com

ISBN-13: 9781662524530 (hardcover)
ISBN-13: 9781662524554 (paperback)
ISBN-13: 9781662524547 (digital)

Cover design by Erin Fitzsimmons
Cover image: © Bogdan Rosu Creative / Adobe Stock; © Smile Shot,
© Master1305 / Shutterstock

Printed in the United States of America

First edition

For Gemma and Asher, with love

Prologue

A s with all fires, this one started small.
A burning bush, if you will.

(Not to get too biblical or anything.)

The plan, if you could call it a "plan," was simple: a controlled fire to burn the evidence.

Now, *control* was a word these LA women—all mothers of private, progressive, constructivist elementary school children—knew well because the struggle was real . . . *for them*. And these women had seen enough Shonda Rhimes shows to understand they needed to cover up the evidence, to conceal the murder.

But *was* it a murder?

Murder was such an extreme and, frankly, polarizing word, so they tried to avoid using it. This was an accidental death. For the most part.

It was definitely a death. That was something they could all agree upon.

Whatever they called it—and they did hesitate to label anything because "Label is libel"—a corpse lay there, along with some other incriminating evidence, and these women knew they each had a motive (or multiple motives); they had each behaved badly, so very badly, so they could each be held responsible or accountable in some way; and none of them trusted the others to tell the truth or uphold the lie. So they did what they assumed anyone in their position would do: burn it all down.

The fire—as fires do—spread quickly, nothing *controlled* about it, and the women ran away faster than a sprint in a Peloton tread class.

What none of them noticed at the time was the bloodstained vintage L.L.Bean flannel hanging from a tree branch, the only piece of evidence that might ultimately survive and could possibly spark suspicion.

The women seamlessly blended into the trail of expensive hybrid SUVs and Teslas, leaving the Southern California glampground that night as it burned behind them, ending what was supposed to have been a weekend of celebration and healing for the Palms School community.

For many, the fact that someone might end up dead at the annual glamping trip didn't actually seem that far-fetched. Taking city people (from Los Angeles, no less!) into the woods was basically begging for murder.

But we're getting ahead of ourselves, aren't we?

THE PALMS SCHOOL MISSION STATEMENT

Inclusive of a multicultural, anti-racist community of experiential learning and critical, compassionate thinking, the Palms School is devoted to progressive learning and respecting children's individuality by challenging our students to discover meaning and significance in the world around them while also preparing them to impact the world as educated, thoughtful, inquisitive, kind, philanthropic global citizens for a lifetime.

Est. 1995

PART I

Back to School Night

Milly

September was hands down Milly's favorite month of the year. Why? Because her kids went back to school. Also, it meant summer was coming to an end, and Milly loathed hot weather. Her fair skin burned just contemplating the sun, and while she had a joy-sparked walk-in closet full of expensive, chic wide-brimmed hats, she somehow always managed to get sun poisoning somewhere. Also, her facialist would be furious with her if she had even a hint of sun exposure, and she did not want to piss off Svetlana or she'd get bumped from her much-coveted standing monthly appointment.

What she'd learned when she moved to LA from her native Connecticut twenty years earlier was that September didn't mean the same thing in Los Angeles that it did on the East Coast. Just as women didn't seem to age here, nature was also defied by seasons that refused to change. The leaves didn't turn magical shades of autumnal colors. And somehow September was now hotter than August.

Maybe she should blame climate change? Her family had started composting (she posted about it on Instagram!), so she knew she was part of the solution and not the problem, but she also knew there was more she could be doing to save the planet, and she often made a mental note to work harder on that but also . . . not be too hard on herself?

While Milly was "just a mom" in the summer months—hiding under hats and sequestering in the air-conditioning of her open-plan, two-story, fully renovated Spanish-style home in Hancock Park—in

September, Milly became class mom and president of the PTA, and this fall, in what some might call an elementary school–leadership coup, Milly had also been named head of the fundraising committee.

It was a trifecta of epic proportions.

Milly took these roles seriously. She knew some of the "working moms" thought of her as "just a mom" regardless of all her titles and hard work.

Did that bother her?

Not really.

Maybe a little.

Okay. More than a little.

It drove her fucking nuts, if she was honest about it.

It made her want to *KILL* them!

Okay, not really, like, commit *murder*, obviously. But . . . weren't women supposed to be leaning in? If they learned nothing else from Sheryl Sandberg and her journey from her gorgeous book—which Milly had read almost three full chapters of and which still, years later, graced her bedside table as a reminder that one day she would finish reading it—shouldn't it be that?

She knew that the work she did for the Palms School was—or hopefully would be, definitely *should* be—appreciated. And tonight was the night she waited for all year with both anticipation and a touch of anxiety:

Back to School Night.

A night when she would reintroduce herself to the Palms community as the new head of the annual fundraising campaign.

The Palms School, nestled in the heart of Hollywood, didn't look like much. It was an "urban school," and by *urban*, she did not mean *Black*. Though of course all colors and religions were welcome at the Palms (and not just *welcome* but essential to the multicultural fabric of the school!). No, she literally meant *urban* as in *city*.

Wait. Was she allowed to say that? Was she allowed to think that? She honestly wondered, but would never—could never—ask it aloud. Who would she even ask, anyway? There were ears everywhere. It seemed like everyone was listening. Maybe not the way she was "listening," which was *listening to learn*, but y'know—*listening*.

The Palms School was known—nay, renowned (in certain circles)—for its warm, progressive, constructivist education and community, and for raising and educating the next generation of kindhearted, inquisitive, anti-racist global citizens. When facilitating tours for prospective parents, Milly always made sure to point out that private middle schools in Los Angeles *loved* Palms elementary kids and they were known for getting *all* their students into their first-choice private middle schools.

She always felt a sense of acceptance and purpose when she pulled up to the school and into her dedicated parking spot in the lot. She had won it in the school's silent auction the year before. (She later learned she had been bidding against herself, but the $10K was well worth it, as it obviously all went to the school and assured her a parking spot, which—ask anyone—is priceless in LA, especially when the school parking lot had been under construction for the last two years for the new Field of Dreams project she had helped spearhead.)

But now was not the time to think about her parking spot. Now she would have to speak in front of all the parents and teachers and school administrators, namely to get families to give more to the beleaguered Field of Dreams project, which had gone way over budget. But here was where it got tricky: she also needed families to donate to the annual Giving Campaign with the goal of 100 percent participation. These contributions were expected *on top of* the tuition they all paid. It was the Cirque du Soleil of fundraising, and Milly had dedicated her entire summer to perfecting her speech.

"Hello, Palms parents!" she began. "I'm Milly. And a lot of you know me because I wear many hats at this school."

Wait for it.

"Even a beret, sometimes."

Silence. Like, she could have actually heard a pin drop.

The parents in the room stared at Milly with polite smiles. Milly shifted in her Chloé scallop-edged flats. She should have worn boots.

"Tranquila," she said to herself, like her beloved El Salvadoran nanny, Guadalupe, would say to her kids.

"I've been a room parent for seven years. So yes, I'm the author of all those emails! I know you working moms will be relieved to hear that I moved you to BCC this school year. You're welcome, ladies!"

Another awkward silence. She'd meant it as a joke, but it was based in truth. There had been a lot of complaints about those who replied all. Personally, Milly was a fan of "reply all." Why have it as an option if not to use it? And she loathed the term *spare your inbox*. It wasn't like their inboxes were sentenced to *murder* by a couple of class emails . . . *about their children.*

"I'm the mother of a fourth grader and a second grader—or, as my husband would say, 'the Mother of Dragons.'"

A few laughs. Some parents shifted in their seats. She was losing them and she had just started. She had told her husband she shouldn't use that "Mother of Dragons" line. *Game of Thrones* was, like, a thousand years ago, and no one she knew watched the spin-off. Why did she ever ask for help on these speeches? She had to remember she was perfectly capable of doing it herself.

Silence. Then, a forced laugh and applause. Milly looked up to see it was coming from a mom who had just arrived, a mom whom no one expected to see again. An impeccably coiffed woman named Dawn, who was trailed by her "problematic" husband.

Parents looked over to see the couple and audibly gasped. The tension in the room was palpable.

For most parents in the community, this was the first time they were seeing Dawn since her family had left the country years ago, when her husband was very publicly fired from his own law firm and "MeToo'd." Or canceled. Or both. Milly couldn't keep track of the appropriate verbiage, but she knew she didn't want her or her own husband to be either of those things or they would be personas non grata in

Hollywood, and her husband's many trendy bars and restaurants relied completely upon being in everyone's favor.

When Milly had learned about Dawn's family's return in confidence earlier that week, she'd been surprised that the Palms would let their family back in, but she also knew, as fundraising chair, the school needed the money, and Dawn's family could pay to be there. And then some.

Milly knew it wasn't Dawn's fault that they'd had to leave, and no one knew exactly why her husband had been fired (though it was common knowledge he had a temper), but she still felt they should have just stayed in Canada. And would it have killed her to arrive on time that night instead of staging this big surprise entrance that interrupted the speech Milly had been preparing for months?

Tranquila.

Milly realized she was still reading, still talking, words were coming out of her mouth, but her mind was elsewhere.

Tranquila.

Heather

September was always a hard month for Heather: it marked the anniversary of the birth and death of her first child. She loved her other child, who was healthy—and for that, she was grateful. But she also felt entirely entitled to have him after the traumatic loss of her first.

She often wondered what her first child would have been like had he lived. And sometimes, and she would never admit this to anyone, when her son was acting particularly bratty, she would think that if her first baby had lived, he never would have behaved like this. It wasn't helpful. And she knew that. She still thought it. She probably always would. But she felt strongly that therapy was a waste of time and money, so that was not something she did.

Now September would be even worse for Heather: it was the month that Dawn and her husband reappeared in Los Angeles and in the Palms community. Heather had to do a double take when they walked in late to Back to School Night.

Dawn's dark hair was swept back into a perfect ponytail, not a wisp out of place. She had what Heather called "resting smile face," the opposite of "resting bitch face," which Heather had been accused of having her entire life and, frankly, was fine with.

Heather obviously knew why they had left years before, and let's just say she had not missed them. And the truth was, it was partly—mostly—Heather's fault. When Heather had complained to HR about Dawn's husband, he was forced out of the firm. Of course, there were many other flags in his file. Dawn's husband, while meek looking, had a real temper. Everyone knew that. He was that guy in the (cheapest) Tesla who made a left into the carpool line (strictly forbidden), effectively cutting off two blocks of cars that had been lined up, patiently waiting (as per the clearly laid out rules that everyone else followed) for ten minutes. And then *took a left* out of the carpool, running over the bright-orange cone with the huge sign that read NO LEFT TURN.

What an asshole.

She'd thought the whole drama with Dawn's husband would be behind them once their family moved to Canada, but now they were back? Another mom whispered to her that she'd heard they were staying with Dawn's in-laws in Encino. Living with in-laws in the Valley? A fitting punishment, Heather thought.

The other moms in the Palms community loved gossiping and talking about food and dieting and perimenopause and the importance of mental health. Heather loathed the notion of oversharing about anything. She was not a "girl's girl." If she heard about one more mom sneaking samples of Ozempic, she was going to scream into her down-alternative pillow.

What? She had allergies.

Heather had grown up in a small town in Idaho, and was built like a whippet, like all the women before her, but was not immune to weight gain in her forties, though she would never admit it to anyone. It was, quite simply, no one's business.

Heather sat in the back of the multi-multi-multipurpose Palms gym/auditorium/etc., watching this woman, Milly, talk about fundraising and just *flailing*. What was she even going on about? For sure, she was one of those moms who replied all. And why was she so nervous? Why was she standing on her tiptoes? Heather thought Milly should have worn boots; then maybe she'd feel more grounded. Heather always wore boots when she had an important meeting, which was most days.

Heather wondered how long this event would go on for. She usually played live ball at the tennis club on Monday nights, and she was annoyed to have to miss it.

The tennis club was her happy place, where she was able to get her aggression out on the court. She liked tennis because she was good at it and she didn't need to depend on anyone but herself to win. There was no one to blame for failure and no one to steal her glory.

She also had a brief to write and about a hundred emails to return. She'd billed only eight hours that day, and she wanted to get ahead of the week. She also hated to pay the sitter to watch her son so she could attend a school function—a school for which they were paying $25K a year, before donations.

She, after all, had gone to public school in Idaho, and she'd turned out fine. The dirty little secret was that she made more money than her husband, who'd gone to "the best private schools." Still, guess who always whipped out the credit card when they went out to dinner with another couple? The husbands.

Patriarchal bullshit.

Speaking of bullshit, when was this going to be over?

Dawn

They were back in Los Angeles. Thank-fucking-God.

Fine. They weren't in Los Angeles per se. They were in Encino. Living with her in-laws. It wasn't ideal, no, but it was a step. A big step. A long, graceful leap toward normalcy.

Dawn had a five-pronged plan (she lived for plans and lists):

> Get their son back into the Palms School. Check!
>
> Get back to Los Angeles. Check! (Encino was close enough for now.)
>
> Get her husband's consultancy business up and running. Check! He was scrappy, and that was *one of the many reasons* why she'd married him (she had a list for why she'd married him too).
>
> Get more (okay, *any*) clients for her life-coaching company, It's Always Darkest Before the Dawn. (She had a knack for puns and combining words.)
>
> Get off the wait list (different kind of list—one she didn't love) and into the tennis club!

They had been on the wait list at the tennis club since she was pregnant with her son. While they were living in Canada, they heard their spot had moved up and they would be considered for membership if they were still interested in joining. The tennis club was everything to Dawn. It was her happy place. And it now had pickleball, which she had become really good at in Canada! She loved everything about tennis and clubs, and she knew her husband wanted it more than anything. Her husband was an exceptional tennis player. He'd played for Duke. Although he'd been kicked off the team when his court behavior was likened to "a less skilled, more whiny McEnroe."

She took the club membership as a sign: Los Angeles was ready for their return. And the Palms was eager for tuition-paying families, as they were trying to complete the new Field of Dreams.

Okay, so a lot of people in the Palms community were surprised they were back. The reality was that, sure, Dawn's husband had fucked up—he was human. But did that mean they had to be excommunicated from their school and community? Didn't anyone remember the parable of the prodigal son, for God's sake?

The Woke Mob was obviously to blame, but she knew their family had to play nice now. Extra nice. Sure, they could have stayed in Canada with her family, if not for her husband burning bridges there too. That was another story. And it was especially surprising because her husband had been such a prize when she met him. She was thirty-one at the time and had gone through seemingly every heterosexual male on Match.com (and Hinge, and maybe some others) in the greater Los Angeles area.

She ended up meeting her husband the old-fashioned way: at a single friend of a single friend's new girlfriend's Breaking of the Fast on Yom Kippur. Of course, Dawn didn't actually fast. She "ate light," like she did every day. As a survivor of anorexia in her teens, fasting on Yom Kippur would be for the wrong reasons . . . and quite frankly, triggering. She had her own relationship with God and preferred to atone in her own way: on her Peloton bike. Also, she was only half-Jewish, and it was on her dad's side.

And now here they were, living with her in-laws in Encino and staring at Heather, the woman who had tried to ruin their lives. What Dawn wanted to say to Heather was *You know why your baby died?*

Because he didn't want to spend one day with you as his mother. She had fantasized about saying it to her face since she found out that Heather was the one who had gotten her husband fired, thereby upending their lives. But she was so embarrassed and disgusted by this fantasy (and a few others) that she didn't dare say them out loud, even to her shrink, whom she *loved*. (Her shrink looked like Nora Ephron and always told her to be easier on herself. It didn't matter that she wasn't on her health insurance plan, because mental health was worth it.)

Still, this woman—Heather—had tried to ruin their lives and livelihood, and now she was just sitting there across the room from her, in her skinny jeans and her naturally straight hair, and it took a lot of restraint for Dawn to not go slap her across the face.

Here's the thing: Dawn was a good person. She loved their school community and really believed in everything the Palms School stood for. In the wake of George Floyd, Dawn had marched along Melrose for Black Lives Matter, long enough to post a selfie on social media. She'd also posted I'm listening, and shared books written by Black authors about how to not be racist.

But if she was being honest, she hadn't actually read them. Not because she didn't believe in them, but just because, truthfully, Dawn didn't love nonfiction. Unless it was written by a Royal. And even then, she preferred to listen to it rather than read it. When listening to *Spare*, she would close her eyes and imagine "H" talking directly to her, whispering his story in her ear. She wanted to mother him and fuck him all at once.

Didn't everyone?

Dawn genuinely wanted to educate herself on racism, not just post about it on social media, but she also didn't want to spend the money on a book she knew she probably wouldn't finish, and when she had tried to rent the e-book through the library, there'd been a 753-person wait list for the two copies available. She guessed that lots of other woke but frugal people like her also had the best intentions.

Anyway, by the time the book was offered to her from the wait list, she had moved on to another crusade: Adopt, Don't Shop. Which was tricky since she had paid $3K for a purebred labradoodle who now had his own verified Instagram account.

Dawn knew people would be watching her and her family. They all had to play nice. Getting accepted into the tennis club, for Dawn, meant being accepted back into her community, and that, along with getting revenge on Heather by infiltrating her sacred place, was the ultimate goal.

Milly

"I love my work for the school, but my husband worries sometimes I take on too much. And that's when I say to him . . ."

Milly had arrived at the most important part of the speech. The mission statement, if you will.

"'Anything for Eva.'"

Milly couldn't help but break into a broad grin. She turned to look—nay, *marvel*—at Eva Miller, the Palms' principal, who had come into her role, fortunately or unfortunately, during the pandemic. During that time, there had been a lot of chatter among the moms speculating that Eva's smooth skin was due to a Zoom filter, but even now, in the fluorescent light of the school multiuse auditorium/cafeteria/gymnasium, her cheeks glowed like a perfectly ripe white peach. Her shoulder-length hair, caramel colored with hints of gray (grays she wore like a badge), framed her round face.

Watching Eva on Zoom during the pandemic had brought Milly tremendous comfort during a time of so many unknowns. She'd looked forward to those virtual town halls, when Eva would talk with confidence, authority, assurance, and passion about the pitfalls of the yard's play structure, masking protocols, and the severity of the newly revised carpool rules.

"So when Eva asked me to preside over the fundraising committee this year, on top of being the mom to two kiddos and room parent and

PTA president, I couldn't help but laugh because I think she knew what I'd say: *Anything for Eva.*"

Some parents laughed. Not a lot. Milly couldn't fully gauge it because she and Eva made eye contact, sending chills down her spine.

It took her a second to catch her breath. But she knew she had to press on with her speech.

"And that's why we're asking for one hundred percent participation in this year's annual fundraising drive!"

Milly realized she was standing on her tiptoes. She lowered herself. She wished again that she had worn boots.

"Because it's the annual fundraising drive that keeps our tuition lower than other schools'."

She was sure she heard a snicker. Parents shifted uncomfortably in their folding chairs.

"And of course, there are so many additional opportunities to give back to our school. The Party Book will be live online tomorrow. And for those of us who are new to the community, the Party Book is a book of parties thrown by Palms parents to raise money for our school . . . and best of all, to foster community and have fun! You should get an email soon with details, but spoiler alert: I'm hosting a sound-bath book party. And if you haven't ever been to a sound bath, trust me, it's like no other bath you've ever had! And it will directly benefit the completion of the Field of Dreams."

Another latecomer noisily entered through the back of the room.

Of course. Jillian.

The clink of a plastic glass. Jillian poured herself a tall glass of wine and reached for a food container. Wait, didn't Jillian Venmo her for only *one* meal? Milly was pretty sure she had seen Jillian's husband receive one earlier.

Jillian pretended to tiptoe to her seat, but her YSL wedges made that impossible—click, clack, click, clack—and now she was waving to people, winking at others. Milly seethed. She knew how much money Jillian and her husband gave every year, and it was insignificant. Last year, they applied for financial aid. Yet here she was, wearing YSL and about to sit right in front of Milly. And then Jillian began whispering to the mom next to her. Milly's confidence wavered.

She could feel a droplet of sweat inching down her back toward her lace thong. Why had she ever thought writing so much would be a good idea?

She was *exhausted*.

But she had to keep talking. *Focus, Milly. Anything for Eva.* She should have taken a beta-blocker. She needed water. And, like, a *trough* of tequila.

The fluorescent lights flickered, and she started seeing spots. She couldn't see Eva. *Where did she go? Drink. Have a drink of water. Drinking.*

It was so quiet. No one was talking or laughing. They were waiting for her to finish drinking. She wished she hadn't worn these flats, because her ankles were shaking and she was sure they'd give out.

Jillian

Tuition lower than other schools? Ha! It seemed both ironic and fitting that Jillian should enter the Back to School Night event at this point in Milly's speech.

Jillian was late. Her husband was there already . . . and, ugh, why would he sit right in front? She really couldn't trust him with a single decision. She should have let him park the car so she could choose where they sat, but the reality was, she was the better driver, and she got carsick when he drove. Her shrink said it was a control thing, but Jillian was pretty sure it was just because her husband rode the brakes too much.

Also, she really wasn't in the mood to socialize with the other parents in the Palms community.

It was a lot to handle this year with her husband *still* unemployed. And they were in the process of submitting their daughter's applications to private middle school, knowing they couldn't afford it and wouldn't receive a scholarship from anywhere because her daughter had "learning differences" and was generally "unexceptional" (according to the Palms' principal, Eva Miller).

Yes, Eva had actually said that.

Unexceptional.

When Jillian's daughter had been diagnosed with ADHD and dyslexia two years earlier, Jillian was told that they were not called "disabilities" anymore; they were called "learning differences," although to Jillian, who, on top of private school, had to spend money on an educational therapist and a psychiatrist to prescribe the right medication for the ADHD, it sure felt like a disability. Or at least a disadvantage. So even though their daughter was a great kid—the greatest kid: outgoing and kind and smart and pretty goddamned special and exceptional, if you asked her—what was that worth when it came to an "unexceptional" white girl with learning "differences" applying for private school admissions where the main question was "How will your family contribute to our commitment to diversity, equity, inclusion, and belonging?"

Jillian thought about when everything happened with George Floyd in 2020. She and her husband had read blogs and parenting articles on how best to talk to their kids about it. She didn't want to get it wrong. They discussed it as a family. They went out in their manicured front yard and held flashlights in the sky and were silent for eight minutes to represent the eight minutes that Floyd was denied oxygen. She understood the irony of it, the privilege they had; she felt crushing guilt about it all, but she was trying. Honestly trying. She wanted her kids to be better than she was. She wanted that for them, and for the world.

Then, without her and her husband's prompting, their daughter had changed her TikTok account photo to a simple graphic with the letters *BLM*, and their younger son, who was on a *Minecraft*-related text chain with all his buddies, also changed their group-chat name in solidarity. These were little things, of course, but they were something.

Unfortunately, the boys were still spelling phonetically, so upon closer look, their group-chat name read *Black Lives Madder*. The parents caught it quickly, and some saw humor in it, but mostly they were embarrassed and helped the boys understand the difference between *matter* and *madder*.

The young kids had the best intentions. Still, Jillian thought, these were a bunch of privileged white boys sitting at home, playing *Minecraft* online during a global pandemic. The Black Lives Matter movement was about as real to them as the game they were playing. Maybe less.

If you asked Jillian what she hated most about herself, she'd ask you how much time you had. First of all, she was entitled—it was in her DNA somehow. She hated that about herself, but she couldn't seem to exorcise it, no matter how hard she tried or how much therapy she did. She always felt that she was supposed to be—was *meant* to be—more successful in her career; married to someone wealthier, more fabulous, more of a baller, more more more everything than her husband had turned out to be. Though, as Jillian's mother liked to point out to her passive-aggressively, "He was doing quite well when you married him." Like somehow her husband's career spiral was her fault?

While this may have been unfair for her mother to say, her husband's career *had* taken a nosedive after they got married. Fifteen years later, they were both still wondering where he went wrong. She would never begrudge her friends their achievements or the accomplishments of their spouses, but she often found herself consumed by a crippling mix of physical and emotional envy for their financial comfort and their generous expense accounts.

It had been more than a decade of ups and downs, years of her husband *almost* getting *the* job that would put his career—and thus, their marriage and family finances—back on track. And every time it had seemed like he was going to get a particularly exciting job, and Jillian was trying to tell the universe they were ready for it . . . to meet the universe where it was at . . . she would put a beautiful bottle of Veuve (a gift from who knows when—she certainly did not buy it) into the refrigerator to chill.

Refrigerating the Veuve felt hopeful. Seeing it in the door of the fridge was, in itself, a reminder that anything could happen. They were just one *yes* away from success. This was Hollywood, after all.

But after a while, that bottle of Veuve in the door of the refrigerator seemed to mock her and the life she felt entitled to have.

When inevitably her husband didn't get the job that would put his career and their marriage back on track, she would numbly take the bottle out of the refrigerator and put it back in storage. She wondered if Champagne could skunk the way beer did. Or was that just a collegiate cautionary tale so everyone would keep drinking?

Sometimes the job-interview process would go on for months, or the job would disappear, or worse, she would order too much almond milk from Costco and there just wouldn't be room for the bottle of Veuve in the refrigerator.

That's what happens when you buy in bulk: you may have the essentials you need at a fair price, but you also may give up room for hope.

Most recently, she'd given the bottle of Veuve as a gift to the Palms' principal, Eva Miller. She'd wanted to make a good impression and start the school year off on the right note. Eva had said thank you, but Jillian felt like she didn't mean it.

Jillian would be lying if she said she hadn't tried on several outfits before deciding on her casual high-waisted jeans, tight sweater, and black YSL suede wedges. On the heels of the pandemic, in which her only fashion investments were more Target sweatpants, she knew she had to step it up for the school's first Back to School Night in years, but she also couldn't look like she was trying so hard. She had been a mom at this school since her daughter was eighteen months old, starting Parent & Me classes before ultimately being accepted into the preschool and then the elementary school after that.

Did she apply for her daughter to attend the bigger, better elementary school for kindergarten, the school with the real field, and where most eight-year-old birthday parties were hosted in the ballroom of the Four Seasons Hotel in Beverly Hills with personalized swag? She sure did. Did she get in? She sure didn't. Did she convince herself that she hadn't tried hard enough to get in and that if she had tried harder and called upon more people to vouch for them, they would have gotten in?

Yes.

Her excuse was that her daughter loved the Palms and that their family was part of the community, and so it was the right school. Which may have been true. It still drove her nuts that their gala was held in the school's multipurpose room with three dads playing nineties covers when the other school had Beyoncé and Jay-Z performing at the Ebell Theatre.

And the worst part? The gala tickets for the two schools cost the same!

(Though to be clear, only at the other school did they auction off a purebred golden retriever puppy for $20K to a prospective family who then did *not* get into the school a month later. Jillian, who often felt more sympathy for dogs than humans, wondered if that beautiful, sweet puppy would become a living, breathing, drooling reminder to those parents of their failure to get their child into their school of choice.)

But the harshest reality that Jillian struggled to accept was this: while she'd grown up fancy in New York City and gone to *the* private school in Manhattan, it really didn't mean shit in Los Angeles. Here, she was fancy adjacent at best.

So she leaned into self-deprecating and funny, reminding everyone she had peaked decades ago. In her late forties, she still led with the fact that she'd gone to an Ivy League school and that she'd gotten into Stanford but turned it down.

She would say, "I studied education in college," but really she'd taken the Intro to Education course, in which she and four other white, privileged Ivy League women created a detailed prototype for a diversity-forward charter school. Now that kind of liberal idealism she had always espoused and embraced and touted and truly believed in was quite literally ruining her life, or at least ruining the life she'd expected—or felt entitled—to have. But she could never say that out loud. She shouldn't even be thinking it.

When Jillian had voiced her concerns to Eva about her daughter getting into a private middle school, given the competition and diversity-forward landscape of private school admissions and her daughter's learning differences, Eva unsympathetically asked, "Isn't that question the definition of white privilege?" Jillian didn't know how to answer and had left the meeting feeling angry, ashamed, and helpless.

So, as Jillian was now suddenly faced with writing her daughter's private middle school applications, would she lead with the political activism of her now-deceased immigrant in-laws, who'd died penniless and in debt, in a country that wasn't their own?

The irony, if you could call it that, was that it was her in-laws' immigrant status that *might* help get her daughter admitted to the school because she was "first-generation American," but it was her comfortable, white fourth-generation-American parents—whom she wouldn't mention anywhere in the application—who would pay the hefty $50K (plus!) annual price tag of tuition because Jillian and her husband couldn't afford it themselves.

Jillian recognized that it was Machiavellian as fuck, but the truth was, *so was the private school admissions process.*

Jillian wholeheartedly and emphatically believed in the diversity and inclusion initiative in schools, and wanted her daughter to go to a school with the aforementioned diversity and inclusion. But Jillian also wanted her "unexceptional" daughter with "learning differences" to get into one of these private schools.

It was a real woke white woman's catch-22, and Jillian recognized the irony but still lost sleep over it.

As for Eva, Jillian never liked her. Her earnestness. Her smugness. Her moral superiority. Her bullish confidence that so clearly masked her insecurities. Her defensiveness, and her inability to admit her mistakes. Her utter lack of humor. Worst of all, she held the key to getting Jillian's daughter into private middle school for seventh grade, and she knew it, and she held it over her. Jillian resented Eva for that.

It didn't help that Eva's daughter was also in sixth grade and would be vying for the same private school spots as Jillian's daughter. That also infuriated her. It didn't seem fair.

Fair.

What did that even mean?

Jillian stopped to get a glass of wine and a cheese plate. She wasn't hungry, but she felt she should take one because somewhere along the way with tuition and donations, she was sure she had paid for it, so someone should enjoy it. From across the room, seated near Jillian's husband, her friend Alice, a fellow "working mom," held up her empty plastic glass and shook it at Jillian. Jillian acknowledged her with a nod and a wink, poured another glass, and juggled it all as she made her way over.

Alice was a friend, and also a good customer of Jillian's. Because in order to supplement her and her husband's mediocre/nonexistent incomes, Jillian sold her daughter's extra Adderall/Vyvanse/QuilliChew/ etc. to moms in the Palms community. It was a pretty recent endeavor, since after her daughter's diagnosis with ADHD, they had tried no fewer than ten different types of stimulants before finding one that didn't make her sick.

The "business" had started over the summer when the kids were at sleepaway camp. Jillian had had a little too much rosé and joked about giving out pills to her friends before they expired. The women hadn't thought she was joking at all, and independently went back to her for more.

And they were willing to pay.

She got paid from the other moms through Venmo and Zelle—the descriptions were creative, if a bit cloyingly on the nose: Teacher's gifts, Team Snacks, Vitamin A, all of which were followed by a wink or kiss emoji, though of course she preferred cash.

Her husband didn't know, which was fine. She handled all the money, anyway, and she knew he would disapprove. His sense of morality and honesty were two of the things she'd fallen in love with almost two decades ago. Now they just annoyed her, like almost everything else about him, which caused her crushing guilt.

And yet she did still love him. Marriage was so fucked up that way.

As Jillian walked through the seated rows of parents, she did a double take when seeing Dawn and her canceled husband. They were back from Canada? Ugh. Was she still trying to be a life coach or something? Jillian had always been clear that she had more issues with society itself than with the women who were "just moms." At school events, she hated having to ask women, "Do you work?" No one ever asked the dads that. With them, it was always, "And what do you do?" or "Where do you work?" or "Are you in the business?"

In LA, there was really only one business that mattered.

With the moms, these introductions were a dance of sorts, because you didn't want to shame a "full-time mom" by suggesting that her role as "just a mom" wasn't work.

And then there were the working moms who "did it all," pumping out three or four kids while breastfeeding and wearing fabulous shoes and also working, thereby making everyone else look . . . mediocre. Jillian knew these women: they had demanding jobs, were often the breadwinners in their families (which she was now, too, but not by choice), but they also volunteered at school and kept their marriages exciting by blowing their husbands in public bathrooms like the one at Mozza (the pizzeria, not the osteria) on their anniversary. But only on their anniversary. And only in the handicapped bathroom, which was a single bathroom with its own lock so no one could actually walk in and catch them. So, not that much of a transgression, but enough to share with other mom-friends over a bottle of rosé to make the rest of them feel like their marriages were lacking spontaneity.

That was about the point in the moms-only drinks date when someone shared a *give 20 percent, get 20 percent off* code for organic CBD-infused lube for those who would actually admit to not getting wet for their husbands anymore, or that they were going through perimenopause and vaginal dryness is *real*. Jillian had used that 20 percent code and ordered the CBD lube because everyone else was, and in case she and her husband ever had sex again.

Jillian wondered if she'd ever actively *want* to have sex again. She joked with her friends that she was "dead from the waist down." And it wasn't that she just didn't want to be touched by her husband; she didn't want to be touched by *anyone.* She felt that part of her life, sexuality itself, was just . . . over. She was forty-eight, and she was ready to hang up her vagina.

After the first week of school, and the email fight she had with her daughter's teacher over his inability to respect her daughter's accommodations for her learning differences—*Flynn*, who she could only imagine was an inexperienced loser the school had hired since so many of their teachers had left the previous year because Eva was a terrible principal—Jillian had to show up here, not just send the B team (i.e., her husband). Because, let's be honest, at school stuff, and a lot of other stuff, these male humans were next to useless no matter how hard they tried and how much their wives were told by their expensive couples therapists to "empower them" and "share the mental load."

Her husband did not know the term *mental load.*

Jillian couldn't help but laugh imagining the inner dialogues of the dads who had been forced to come and were staring at their phones or at the ceiling or at their feet, wondering how and why they were there and what anyone was talking about and why they had to eat falafel for dinner and whether there would be dessert and what the score was on that sporting event they weren't watching.

She needed to meet this new teacher who held her daughter's educational future in his little tattooed Gen Z hands. He would, after all, be tasked with writing her daughter's recommendation, and his online introduction to the Palms community had come without a bio. Classic Palms move, trying to slip in the hire with zero info.

Eva should have known better than to introduce a new teacher into the Palms community without sharing any information outside of *Loves to hike in his spare time!* It was asking for trouble. And Jillian felt sure trouble was what Eva would get.

"And without further ado, it's time to introduce our fearless leader—principal, *legend*, and my personal hero . . . Eva Miller."

As parents clapped, Jillian watched Milly shakily take her many pages and her water and move away from the podium. Eva clapped as she walked over to Milly.

Milly went for a hug, but Eva shot her hand out for a firm handshake, and it was awkward but classic Eva, and an icebreaker for the audience of parents, who held their breath to hear what she had to say.

When Eva finally ascended to the microphone, she took a moment to look out among her subjects. She pursed her lips, which Jillian guessed was her version of a smile. She was taking it all in. Her power. Her sovereignty. Her vassals staring up at her, silently begging for her approval. It made Jillian sick. Mostly because she was just another one of them, who wanted—nay, *needed*—her approval.

"Good evening, Palms parents, faculty, and staff, and welcome to a new school year! I am thrilled to see you all in person, and not over Zoom."

Eva did her best to smile. Jillian laughed to herself, thinking that Eva might experience actual discomfort from the effort. She knew warmth did not come naturally to the woman.

"As fellow parents of a sixth grader, Mags and I are excited to be on this educational journey with you. As principal of the Palms School, I am thrilled to lead you into and through this school year."

"And now, I will part the Red Sea!" Jillian whispered to Alice, who stifled a laugh as Jillian discreetly passed her a snack-size Ziploc baggie of Ritalin under the table.

Alice winked at Jillian and pulled out her phone. A moment later, a Venmo notification went off on Jillian's phone, prompting a dirty look from Eva.

Jillian tried to charmingly make light of it and mouthed, *Sorry!* when what she really wanted to do was give Eva the fucking bird.

"First things first," Eva continued. "*Thank you*, Milly. I couldn't do it without you. We're all so grateful for everything you do for the school, for our kids, and for us parents. We're so lucky to have you as such a vital and generous part of our community. Can we please give this amazing woman a hand?"

As the people in the room clapped, Milly blushed and put her hands together in prayer, bowing just the slightest bit. Jillian elbowed Alice as they clapped along with everyone else.

"As Milly mentioned . . . the Field of Dreams. We're almost there! I know you've all contributed over the last two years and have been *mostly* patient with the construction and traffic and lack of play space for your children, but the good news is, we're in the homestretch. And we really rely on your continuing generosity to help us fund the finishing of the Field of Dreams, so please, dig deep. The ribbon-cutting ceremony is next month, and we need your dollars to make that happen, to give our kids more space to play and grow. Yes, I want you to think about your own kids, their well-being and physical health, when you contribute to the field—but I also implore you to think about the kids who come after yours. Pay it forward. That's what our Palms community is known for.

"And I wanted to share an exciting new opportunity we're offering: for families who contribute five thousand dollars or more, your kids will get their handprints in the cement by the field. I don't know about you, but I've always wanted to put my hand in wet cement."

Jillian wondered if she was the only one who was horrified by this "opportunity." It certainly did not seem in keeping with the egalitarian mission statement of the school.

"Shifting gears . . . As many of you know, we have welcomed a new sixth-grade teacher to our school community: Flynn Hartshorn. Flynn has always wanted to be a teacher, and while he's admittedly somewhat new to it, we feel he brings an energy and an innovative teaching style to our sixth-grade class. He will be writing recommendations to middle school, and this year, because he is new to the school, I will also be writing my own recommendations for your children and your families."

A hush fell across the audience. None of this was normal. Eva writing the recommendations when her own kid was applying to the same schools? Did anyone else see the conflict of interest? Jillian scanned the room, exchanging looks with other moms.

"So, without further ado, I'd like to introduce our new sixth-grade teacher, Flynn Hartshorn."

It was hard to see his face at first, as parents in the audience craned their necks to see the new teacher who had already sparked so much controversy in the community. He was in the shadows in the back of the multipurpose room, but Jillian could see his outline: tall, broad shoulders, a messy man bun . . . your basic Gen Z nightmare.

He wore knock-off Birkenstock clogs and a T-shirt under a too-tight short-sleeved button-down, which he probably meant to be ironic.

"Mahalo!" he began.

This was even worse than she'd thought. Jillian couldn't believe her daughter's educational future was in this loser's hands.

"Hi, everybody. My name is Flynn Hartshorn. I know, my name sounds like a character from a romance novel."

Some chuckles. Parents wanted to like him. Why shouldn't they?

"Uh, I just moved out here to Los Angeles. I grew up in Arizona. ASU! Anyone?"

Crickets.

"Okay, well . . . in my spare time, I play music and hike. And yeah . . . My pronouns are *he/him* . . . What else?"

A mom across the room raised her hand but didn't wait to be called on before asking her question. "What school were you teaching at before coming to the Palms, and what experience do you have in progressive experiential-constructivist education?"

"Wow. Great questions. Well, I was a substitute teacher for a bit . . . and I, uh, graduated from college and took a gap year before that. I traveled through India and Indonesia. I lived with the monks in the mountains, making olive oil for a few months—cold press is no freaking joke, you guys! So, yeah. It was pretty epic. The truth is, I had never heard of constructivist education before applying for this position on ZipRecruiter, but ironically, it feels very organic to me as a human person and also to my teaching style, which is pretty . . . improvisational!"

"Have you written a recommendation before?" asked a mom who hadn't raised her hand. Eva clocked it and frowned. The mom cowered, immediately realizing her mistake.

"What do you know about the schools our kids are applying to?" asked another. Again, no raised hand. Eva frowned again.

"Do you believe in standardized testing and if all kids should take the ISEEs even though some schools no longer require it?"

"Oh, man," he said. "What's an ISEE?"

Eva moved in swiftly. Flynn took a step back.

"You will all have a chance to get to know Flynn, and I assure you he is perfectly capable of writing your children's recommendations—"

"Isn't that what ChatGPT is for?" Flynn leaned in toward the mic with a smile.

Eva stared daggers at him as she pressed on. "That was a joke, of course. Humor is so essential in our community, and we're grateful to Flynn for both educating your kids and also entertaining them with his sly sense of humor. And with that, please have a glass of wine, schmooze with your fellow Palms parents, and we hope to see you all around the school and at a party-book party soon."

Jillian stared at her phone, not actually reading anything but listening to the conversations around her, as she waited in a long line of moms wanting to get face time with Eva:

"Will you give *more* money to the new field?"

"I can't believe the field isn't done."

"Field of Dreams? More like Field of Nightmares!"

"Did you see Dawn is back from Canada? Wasn't her husband—"

"Don't say the *C* word."

"Canada?"

"No . . . *canceled*."

"Oh."

"So, if we already gave money to the field, will our kids get to do the handprints?"

"My son is allergic to cement, but I'll probably give money anyway just to make sure Eva gives me a good recommendation."

"Why do you think Dawn came back?"

"Maybe her husband got canceled in Canada too?"

"Do you think they tell the schools how much money the families give?"

"Obviously."

"I think that's illegal."

"It's not."

"That Flynn guy has never written a recommendation in his life."

"Maybe to his fraternity?"

"I went to ASU but was too embarrassed to raise my hand."

"Did you see Bella? She's emaciated."

"I know. She looks fabulous."

"She says she's not on Ozempic, but, like, come on."

"You'd think they could have gotten a teacher with more experience for sixth grade."

"I heard there's a teacher shortage nationwide."

"Other schools don't seem to have this problem, though."

"Is it just us?"

"Is it just our kids?"

"It couldn't be. Our kids are great. Right?"

"We should give him a chance, I think."

And as Jillian inched toward the front of the line, Eva excused herself and disappeared.

"Is she coming back?" another sixth-grade mom asked desperately. She looked as rejected and anxious as Jillian felt. But Jillian knew this was how Eva operated, and she wasn't going to waste any more time there tonight, not when they were paying a sitter by the hour to be with their kids.

Jillian grabbed her husband by the elbow and whispered, "Wheels up."

He nodded and they slipped out together. Jillian was proud of herself for having at least one win that night by finding a spot on the street and thus avoiding the long valet line, in which parents had to make idle conversation with each other while they waited for their cars.

Most importantly, Jillian would need to figure out what to do about this new teacher. Did she need to endear herself to him? Or join in on the petitions that other parents were signing to get him removed after he played an episode of *Friends* during social studies class the first week of school?

TO: EVA MILLER
FROM: EVA MILLER
BCC: PALMS PARENTS
Subject: Addressing Community Concerns with Sensitivity

Dear Palms Parents,

It has come to my attention that there is a petition circulating within our community regarding the employment of a new teacher in the sixth grade, citing concerns about their level of experience. I want to assure you that we take all feedback seriously and are committed to ensuring the best possible learning environment for our students.

First and foremost, I want to emphasize our dedication to providing a supportive and inclusive environment for all members of our school community, including our teaching staff. Each member of our faculty brings a unique set of skills and perspectives to the classroom, contributing to the rich tapestry of our educational community.

While I understand that concerns may arise regarding the experience level of our staff, I urge us all to approach this matter with empathy and patience. Transitioning into a new role can present challenges, but it also offers opportunities for growth and development. It is our responsibility as a community to support our teachers as they navigate their professional journey.

As always, the Palms encourages open dialogue and constructive feedback (as long as it is, indeed, constructive) as we work together to address any concerns that may arise.

I want to thank you for your continued support and collaboration as we strive to create a nurturing and inclusive learning environment for all students as well as faculty.

Warm regards,
Eva Miller
Principal, Palms School

TO: MILLY
FROM: MILLY
BCC: PALMS COMMUNITY
Subject: ☀Calling all fabulous Palms Moms! ☀

Leave the chaos of the week behind and treat yourself to a blissful sound-bath experience. Join us for a unique evening of relaxation, rejuvenation, and food from popular eatery Match at a private home in Hancock Park (address upon confirmation of purchased ticket)!

Indulge in the soothing sounds and vibrations that will melt away stress and tension as you connect with fellow moms, unwind, and recharge your mind, body, and spirit.

Also, there will be wine! 🍷

ALL PROCEEDS WILL GO TO FINISHING THE FIELD OF DREAMS!

Limited spots available, so RSVP today to secure your spot! Don't miss out on this opportunity to pamper yourself and enjoy a well-deserved break. Can't wait to see you there! 🌸

XOXO,
Milly

PART II

Sound Bath:

A Party-Book Party Benefiting the Completion of
the Palms School Field of Dreams

Milly

It wasn't the first time Milly had hosted a party-book event that sold out.

The secret?

She enjoyed it!

She did! She fundamentally enjoyed taking care of (most) people. She loved welcoming (most) people into her home. She was immensely proud of the home she had made with her husband. (Of course, it was really *she* who made it, but he—and his bars and restaurants—paid for it.)

It was still an hour before the women were set to arrive, but Milly was already walking around her house, methodically lighting candles. She loved the smell of expensive scented candles—her current favorite was one that had been hand poured in the Hamptons by a celebutante influencer who, upon a deeper dive into her past, actually hailed from New Jersey even though she said she "grew up in New York."

Still, the candle was exquisite.

Tonight, for the sound-bath party-book party ($150 per person—all women), she had bought and arranged hydrangeas and baby's breath. Feminine, chic, understated.

She particularly loved lilies. She used to say they were her "spirit flower," but then Eva had told her that was inappropriate and insensitive language because using the term *spirit* was appropriating Native American culture, which obviously was something she would never dream of doing! So now she just simply said she loved lilies, though she hated that lilies had pollen that would stain, and since her home was essentially fifty shades of beige, she had to hold off on lilies, as much as she loved them.

She likened arranging flowers to what she did in her many roles for the Palms community: taking different varieties of one thing and finding a way to put them together in one vessel to harmoniously coexist. It wasn't a perfect metaphor, but really, what was?

Her kids were allergic to most flowers, which was a problem but not insurmountable if she put them in strategic places where they couldn't get to them.

Milly wondered if maybe her kids wouldn't be so allergic if she had been able to successfully breastfeed them when they were babies. With her first, she'd pumped and pumped, but between her "flat" nipples and constant mastitis, she couldn't keep up with her tiny newborn's voracious appetite. With her second, she didn't even try, opting out of breastfeeding altogether (while keeping it a secret from her mom-friends). She still felt guilt and shame over her inability to breastfeed her children. It was her first, but certainly not her last, failure as a mother.

Stop it, Milly! she told herself. She needed to be more forgiving of herself, she thought as she moved a vase of flowers from the open-plan kitchen island to the vintage bar cart by the glass sliders, which led out to the pool.

She looked over the staging of food on the farmhouse dining table. A server from one of her husband's restaurants had dropped off the pastas and salads earlier that evening. She would, of course, take them out of the silver foil containers (she made a mental note to speak to her husband about not using these containers, which were terrible for the environment) and serve them in her bespoke ceramic bowls and plates made by a Native American woman who lived in Maine. Or was it Vermont? Maybe New Hampshire? How Milly loved supporting diverse women!

Also, her nanny, Guadalupe, would be there to help clean up, of course, after putting her kids to bed. Thank heavens for Guadalupe!

What would she ever do without her? Just thinking about life without Guadalupe made her immediately anxious, and she had to say to herself, "Tranquila."

She had reiterated this "tranquila" mantra earlier when she realized she would have to pivot the party layout due to the rain. The plan initially was to hold the drinks portion of the evening outside in the backyard; they'd had heaters installed into the pergola for this very reason, to entertain even when it got cold at night—LA was the desert, after all! But that would not do in the rain.

Want to make God laugh? Make a plan.

You know who wasn't laughing?

Milly.

Of course, there were last-minute cancellations; people in LA were such lightweights when it came to less-than-perfect weather. And no one ever seemed to know how to drive in the rain. As a girl from Connecticut, Milly found this silly. Sometimes they even canceled school for the rain in LA! Either way, the money they paid for the party-book party was nonrefundable and went straight to the Field of Dreams project, so it was still a win.

But the usual suspects would show up, come hell or high water. These sixth-grade moms were not just coming because they loved sound baths, or even because they knew what a sound bath was. Nor were they coming to support Milly or because she had attended their party-book parties before this. This was not about support for the school, or for the field, or for the art of sound bathing as a niche industry.

No, the goal was as clear as their lasered, facialed, Botoxed skin: they wanted face time with Eva in a casual setting before she wrote their children's recommendations for middle school.

That's right. Everyone knew that Eva would be attending Milly's sound-bath party, and Milly wanted everything to be perfect for her.

And for everyone else, of course.

When the doorbell rang *forty-five minutes early*, Milly assumed it must be FedEx or UPS . . . because *who showed up early to a sound-bath party-book party?*

Milly looked at her Ring camera feed on her phone. It was Dawn. And she was holding something. Milly zoomed in on the video. Oh God, no. Had she brought light-blue *carnations?* In plastic?

She hated Dawn for showing up early. And hated her even more for bringing ugly, cheap flowers. And now Milly would have to put them out, completely ruining her aesthetic, or else she'd seem ungrateful. And she never wanted to seem that way.

Deep breaths. *Tranquila.*

This was *so* Dawn. She tried too hard. Always. Even before her husband was MeToo'd and they moved away. Milly tried to put herself in Dawn's shoes and feel empathy for her and her son. Her son was sweet. In fact, Milly had had him over for a playdate right after their family reappeared at Back to School Night. "Inclusivity" was a major tenet of the Palms community, and Milly wanted to set a good example for her parent peers. So Milly knew that Dawn meant well; she knew she should be more patient with her . . . She was just . . . so . . . underfoot. And Milly had so much to do before Eva . . . and all the other guests . . . started arriving.

She also knew that Dawn was hell-bent on getting into the tennis club. Milly had taken a back seat on the membership committee at the club this year since she had taken on so many extra roles at school, but of course she still had sway, and certainly had a vote. It was probably why Dawn had come early.

What Dawn didn't know? Her membership was going to be rejected. Milly had nothing to do with it, of course, but she had heard that Heather was leading the charge to block Dawn's family and had received the required signatures easily in a single evening of live ball and martinis.

People were terrified of Heather. On and off the tennis court. And in actual court too. She was a lawyer. She was so measured, so blond, so tall, so composed . . . and cold . . . all the time. Milly wondered if Heather might actually be a sociopath, but then she thought that was not "leaning in" and was mean to even think.

Either way, this was not Milly's news to share with Dawn. And she certainly did not want to think about it right now, as she was about to host a party for twenty-plus women in her home, a party to which Heather herself had RSVP'd.

Tranquila.

Milly hugged Dawn, squealing she "shouldn't have," which she meant literally and with every ounce of her being. She told her to relax and sit, but Dawn insisted she was "there to help."

Milly excused herself and went into the powder room, which smelled of rosemary and sandalwood from the New Jersey–celebutante candle. She pulled up her cashmere dress and pulled down her silk underwear, sat on the toilet, closed her eyes, and breathed in deeply as she peed. This was going to be great. Everything would go great. She wondered if she should change into something lighter. She was already sweating. She felt like a fire was burning inside her, and she wondered if this was a hot flash. She hadn't yet had any signs of perimenopause like many of her friends had, but this felt particularly unbearable.

Why was she wearing cashmere? A rhetorical question *obviously*, but fuck if she wasn't way too hot.

She washed her hands with her organic handwash and used one of the paper napkins with gold trim she put out when she was entertaining. She knew these paper napkins were not good for the environment, but her tea towels weren't ironed, so again she'd had to pivot. She would take the dirty napkin with her and throw it out in the kitchen so as not to sully the empty rubbish bin in the bathroom. She kind of saw the irony in that, but also didn't because she had a lot on her mind.

Like a mantra, she repeated her to-do list silently to herself: put the ice in the ice bucket, put out the good crystal stemless wineglasses, unwrap the artisanal snack board, chill the beverages in the ice bath. The mantra played on a loop until—

Milly stepped out from the powder room and noticed . . .

The snack board . . .

Already unwrapped . . .

On a table it should *not* be on.

Fucking Dawn.

She went to it, inspecting it.

A rogue carrot.

A dimple in the hummus.

The beautiful fan of triangle-shaped Manchego cheese slices was askew, as if it were the dairy reimagining of a house of cards that had fallen and been messily reorganized to mask the missing slice.

Milly seethed.

"I'm not sure if that's where you wanted it, but I just wanted to be helpful. I unwrapped it, but I can put it anywhere."

Milly was in such shock that she didn't know how to respond to Dawn. And Dawn, notoriously an enemy of silence, kept talking:

"I just want to be helpful."

Milly clenched her teeth. She wrung her hands.

"I didn't know how long you'd be in the bathroom, so . . ."

If Milly didn't say something, Dawn would just keep talking, and Milly was trying not to scream.

"That's fine. Thank you, Dawn."

Dawn sprang back into action with relief and unbridled enthusiasm. "What else can I do?"

"Relax. You're a guest."

"I just want to be helpful."

"You keep saying that."

The women stood staring at each other for a beat. Dawn opened her mouth to talk, but Milly cut her off.

"Why don't you just sit, Dawn. Have a carrot. Some hummus. Or a slice of Manchego? Or did you already have some?"

Milly knew she was taunting her, but she couldn't help herself. She wanted to see how far Dawn would go.

"Oh, I couldn't."

Milly smiled with her lips closed, burning with rage. "Really?"

Dawn leaned forward and spoke conspiratorially, even though no one else was there to hear her.

"I got some samples of Ozempic from my mother-in-law's bridge partner's son, who is the physician's assistant to a doctor—doctor of what, I have no idea. But anyway, I don't really eat anymore! Also, I'm lactose intolerant."

Milly was furious. She knew Dawn had eaten from that snack board, and now she was doubling down on the lie and the cover-up. Milly went into the kitchen, but as she turned, she ran right into Dawn, who was literally on her heels.

"I was hoping to talk to you about the tennis club," Dawn started. "As you know, we're waiting to hear from the membership committee. Last we heard, when we moved back, it was just a formality, a done deal, but I haven't heard anything since and—"

"I took a back seat on the membership committee this year because of everything I'm doing at school, so I really don't know anything," Milly said.

Not her news to share, she reminded herself. She had a lot of other things on her mind, like hosting this party and making sure everything was perfect for Eva.

Perfect for everyone.

"Oh, come on, Milly. You know everything about everything when it comes to school and the club. When do you think we'll hear?"

Why was Dawn pushing her? Because that's what Dawn did. She pushed and pushed and pushed. *Let it go, Dawn! Read the room!*

Milly looked back at her expensive, bespoke, artisanal, and now compromised cheese board, and back to Dawn, who stared at her expectantly.

Fuck it.

"I'm sorry to be the bearer of bad news . . ." Milly started.

She wasn't.

"It seems like there were some objections . . . to your membership. I don't know if anything is official, of course, but last I heard, it doesn't look good. I'm sorry."

Dawn's chin quivered. And then her mouth closed and opened and closed again. Milly thought if she was quiet enough, she might hear Dawn grinding her teeth.

"But . . . how is that possible? They said it was just a formality."

"I really can't say, Dawn. But there are so many other clubs these days. And a lot of them have pickleball now too. I'm sure you'll find the right club for your family. There are also public courts."

Dawn gasped and her eyes welled with tears.

"*Public courts?* Isn't that where all the homeless encampments are?"

"Dawn, the terminology is *unhoused* now. I'm sure things must be quite different in Canada. I'm so glad you're back! Would you please excuse me?"

Milly moved into the den, where she kept her prescription medication and the Clase Azul tequila. She took an Ativan and a swig from the tall ceramic blue-and-white bottle. Telling Dawn about her rejection from the club wasn't at all as satisfying as Milly had hoped it would be. It was actually kind of sad. And now she felt awful. And guilty. Which wasn't fair, because she hadn't done anything wrong. She was just the messenger! Why had Dawn made her do that?

Tranquila, Milly repeated to herself. Eva would be arriving soon. But not soon enough.

Dawn

Dawn was in shock.

Who . . . What . . . Why would anyone object to Dawn and her family becoming members of the tennis club?

This was not part of her five-pronged plan.

Dawn was reeling. Yes, she had come early to talk to Milly about the club, but she came early to get *good* news, not the awful news she'd received. But also, Dawn had really, truly wanted to be helpful.

Sometimes people say they want to be helpful, but they don't actually mean it. She meant it! Here she was, forty-five minutes early . . . with flowers. They were an impulse buy from a *very nice* lady who was selling bouquets at the light just off the freeway. Dawn felt she could support this woman and also endear herself to Milly. She thought the flowers would be a karmic win-win.

Dawn had never been more sure than she was in that moment: karma was fucking bullshit.

First of all: Milly hadn't seemed grateful *at all* for the flowers. *Spiteful* was the word that came to mind.

Second of all: Was their not getting in the club still about her husband's cancellation? Wasn't everyone past that by now? Didn't anyone believe in redemption? Second chances? Come on!

Third of all: she needed to figure out what had happened. Was Heather behind this? Could Heather be trying to ruin their lives . . .

again? What did they ever do to her? Their sons were friends. Like, really good friends! And Dawn had to lie to her son and make up excuses about why they couldn't have playdates together! It was an unspoken agreement that neither mother would ever communicate with the other.

Fourth of all: Dawn had been underestimated before.

Before her husband's cancellation and their temporary banishment to Canada, Dawn had worked hard to receive her ILCC (International Life Coach Certification). Her son was in preschool, and she wanted to get back into the workplace. What better way than by using her natural leadership skills to help people find their way in this crazy thing we call life?

She had incorporated and called her new company It's Always Darkest Before the Dawn. And her tagline was *For women who want to win at life.*

Dawn was so excited to share this news with the other working moms, who hadn't given her the time of day before that because she was "just a mom." She was sure now they would. She'd offered to do free sessions for them, but none of them had taken her up on it. Very few of them had even emailed or texted or called her back.

When she'd donated a one-on-one life-coaching session to the Palms silent auction and no one bid on it, she was crushed. And then, of course, shortly after that they'd had to leave for Canada.

While Dawn's goal had always been to get back to Los Angeles, she started giving life-coaching tips on Instagram while she was in Canada—using her maiden name, lest anyone trace her back to her husband's disreputable firing—and had managed to get several virtual clients.

Throughout her life, people had always underestimated her. Dawn shared this with her life-coaching clients, who often felt the same way, and she would coach them to use that to their advantage.

She thought of that saying *Fool me once, shame on you. Fool me twice, I will fucking bury you.* Wait, was that how that saying went?

So, Dawn had work to do. She had to get into the tennis club, because say what you want about her—Dawn was determined to win at all costs.

Heather

Heather had agreed to drive Jillian to the sound-bath party but warned her she would not be staying late, so she might have to find another ride home or Uber. Heather prided herself on always being the first to leave a party. Also, everyone knew Jillian had a . . . complicated . . . relationship with alcohol; it was no surprise to anyone that she was canvassing the neighborhood for a designated driver so she could get wasted.

At least she was honest about it. Heather appreciated this about Jillian—it was hard to find something negative to say about her that she hadn't already said about herself.

Drinking wasn't an interest or an option for Heather that night, since she had an important meeting at eight the next morning, and she had already played an hour of tennis so just needed to stay hydrated. But she wasn't going to say no to driving Jillian to the party, because she never knew when she'd need a favor in return. Heather was nothing if not a believer in quid pro quo, professionally and personally. And she didn't mind Jillian's company. She actually found her amusing, though she didn't trust her . . . or any woman, for that matter.

Jillian had asked her in the car why she was going to the party that evening. Jillian said she thought Heather hated stuff like this. Heather had said something like she "wanted to contribute to the field so they could be done with it already." And since this party was benefiting the field, she felt she had to show up.

But that wasn't the truth. Far from it. Heather had been laser focused on keeping Dawn and her family out of the tennis club. It wasn't that hard, actually. Dawn's husband, while a formidable tennis player, was not well liked, and most people felt Dawn was a "climber."

Did she feel some guilt over dashing Dawn's tennis-club dreams? No. She felt more like she was doing a service to her fellow club members by keeping them out, because Dawn's husband was a loose cannon and Dawn was annoying. Everyone thought so.

Heather knew Dawn would be getting the news this evening via email or a call from the head of the membership committee (a woman who had been begging to be Heather's doubles partner for several seasons and now miraculously would be), and Heather wanted to see Dawn's reaction when she heard.

She also wanted to mark Dawn's card, making it clear she'd been responsible for it so Dawn would think twice before encroaching on Heather's territory again. This was important to Heather. She needed boundaries, and those boundaries had to be respected.

It wasn't that Heather wanted to bask in the glow of Dawn's failure. She didn't mind doing that, too, but it was more about her own survival. Heather could not have Dawn's family infiltrating her club. It was bad enough they were back in the Palms community.

What Heather didn't expect—and what kind of annoyed her, frankly—was that Milly had beaten her to it. It was the first thing Milly told her when she arrived that evening.

"Heads up. Dawn knows," Milly whispered into Heather's ear when they were barely through the front door.

"You told her?"

"She wouldn't let it go. You know how she is."

"Does she know I had anything to do with it?"

"I didn't say anything about you. But please, no drama. The sound bath is supposed to be relaxing. And Eva should be here any minute."

Heather rolled her eyes.

"I know, I know," said Milly. "I just had to say it. Please."

Heather saw Dawn in the corner, desperately typing away on her phone. She looked up and their eyes met. Heather smiled smugly. Dawn glared.

Jillian

A lot was riding on tonight's sound-bath party-book party for Jillian. It was an opportunity to talk to Eva in a relaxed, social setting about her daughter and better their chances of getting her into their first-choice school, Redford Prep.

Since Back to School Night, Jillian had finally caved and agreed to have her daughter take the ISEEs—the standardized admissions exam that had become voluntary for most private schools since COVID. Jillian didn't understand how it was helpful for a kid with learning differences to take a standardized test. Sure, she would get a little extra time, but still, it was a standardized test for a kid with an un-standard brain. It felt like it had been set up for her to fail. In her combative call with Eva days before, when she'd pushed back on putting her daughter through the stressful experience (and also having to hire an expensive tutor for an exam that was essentially inadmissible), Eva had lashed out at her, saying, "If she doesn't take it, she's going to think that her mom can get her out of anything she doesn't want to do." Eva also intimated that if she didn't take it, and she didn't get in anywhere, the school would not be to blame.

Since then, Jillian had thought of many great retorts and comebacks to what Eva had said. But they were all too late. She needed a reset with Eva, to make sure Eva knew Jillian had heard her and taken her advice and they were going to do everything Eva had prescribed to get their daughter into her school of choice.

Jillian got a ride to the party with Heather, who was not a scintillating conversationalist, but Jillian appreciated her dryness and complete inability to bullshit. Also, she appreciated not having to drive herself, which meant she didn't have to pay for an Uber and she could relax and drink. She would need it to get through the night.

Her husband, seeing she was getting a ride and not driving herself, cautioned her to "be careful." She hated when he said that. She was a grown-ass woman and mother and wife, who took care of everything, who took on *all* the mental load, *all* the time. So what if once in a while she drank too much? So what if she had a decidedly complicated relationship with alcohol? But then, every few months, there was a night she would, like, kind of black out? Sometimes remembering she had vomited only when she smelled it in her hair the next morning. It was on those mornings that she would truly appreciate her husband. He loved her regardless of her weaknesses and flaws, and she had to feel a little grateful for that.

So, fine. Jillian was a mess, and she knew that. But also, she had a lot going on. All moms did, of course, but Jillian did right now especially.

Milly's house was a little too monotone and precious for Jillian's taste, but it was a choice, and she appreciated that about the decor. Jillian drifted through conversations with other moms, mostly talking about admissions applications and tours; the controversial new teacher, Flynn Hartshorn; and so on. She got sidetracked with one conversation about a new porn site made by women, for women. Her friend Alice gave them a tutorial on setting their browser to "private" so they could surf the porn site freely without the fear of it staying in their history. Watching other Gen X moms trying to figure out private browsing on their iPhones so they could watch female-driven porn was the distraction and entertainment Jillian hadn't known she needed. It felt good to laugh.

Meanwhile, just as it felt like they were all leaning in, some women passive-aggressively discussed whose husbands did and didn't watch porn. Jillian made a mental note not to trust the women who swore their husbands didn't watch it.

She would have much rather continued the porn conversation with the moms who had had a little too much wine already than grovel to Eva, but that was essentially what she was there for, so she had to get to it. She looked around but Eva hadn't arrived yet.

Then, as if she had willed her entrance, Eva walked in the front door. Wading through the women huddled around the snack board, Jillian made a beeline to Eva with as much grace and warmth as she could muster.

Milly

Milly made her way to the door as soon as she saw Eva enter, elbowing Jillian and others out of her way. She was so excited. Finally, Eva had arrived!

What she didn't expect? To see Eva's wife, Mags, with her. Milly tried to keep the warm smile on her face, but when she saw Mags entering behind Eva, she was disappointed. Gutted, actually. Not just that Eva had RSVP'd and paid for only one person and they were obviously two people, but that she would have to share Eva with Mags that night. Milly knew that was ridiculous because Eva and Mags were married. But Milly often joked that she and Eva were "work wives" even though Milly was, at the end of the day, a parent volunteer and not actually employed by the school. It was their bit when they were at school events together, and it made Milly feel like, for those precious moments, she was actually her wife.

"I thought Mags was staying with the kids," Milly whispered to Eva.

"We got a moms' night out," said Eva loudly. "We both wanted to be here, and Mags's mom was happy to babysit. So here we are!"

"Yay!" Milly tried to sound enthusiastic.

Milly side-hugged Mags. She took their coats and hung them on the coatrack she had set up in the hallway. She closed her eyes and tried to regroup. Milly had been so excited about tonight—in particular, sharing it and navigating it and experiencing it with Eva. And now Dawn was upset about the tennis club because of her and Mags was crashing the sound bath, and when Milly came back into the living and dining room area, she was mortified to see moms jockeying for position with Eva so that, at one point, Eva was in a corner, surrounded on all sides by moms trying to get to her.

Milly felt this wasn't fair. To Eva *or* to her. Eva was a guest, and she should be able to enjoy her night in peace.

Milly was spiraling. About Eva. About telling Dawn about the tennis club. She wanted to apologize, but Dawn had excused herself ten minutes ago and hadn't emerged since. Milly knew Dawn had dabbled in bulimia in college, and just hoped she wasn't relapsing in her beautiful, delicious-smelling powder room.

Milly caught her own reflection in the mirror of their entrance hall. What she had done was mean and spiteful. She deserved this for telling Dawn. Also, her makeup looked terrible. Sometimes, recently, when she looked at herself wearing makeup, she thought she looked a little like a sad clown. She tried to shake it off. She knew she looked tired. She had taken on too much. She hadn't made enough time for self-care. But she had to focus on hosting and making everyone feel welcome, whether they were or not.

Women continued to arrive in droves, and cocktail hour was a blur. Milly, the dutiful, seasoned hostess, poured glasses of wine, took coats, chatted briefly with everyone, trying desperately to look comfortable and in control while also being relaxed and, at least seemingly, "having fun!" She tried not to stare at Eva.

Milly was pretty sure she saw Jillian slipping Alice some kind of pills. She'd heard that Jillian sold Adderall and other stimulants to the Palms mommunity, but she didn't really believe it. Maybe it was true?

When Seraphina, the sound-bath singer/performer/leader(?) arrived, Milly greeted her warmly while wishing she could pull off that effortless bohemian-chic vibe. Milly asked her to please get her audience's attention and begin. It was eight thirty already, which, on a school night, felt like midnight.

The women piled into the beige-on-beige-on-white-on-beige living room. They assumed their positions on the immaculate custom velvet sectional—with throw blankets and throw pillows *thrown* just so.

Candles flickered on the mantel over the raging wood-burning fireplace. (Milly felt strongly that gas fireplaces were for lazy philistines.)

Her houseplants were tended to weekly by Arturo, a plant specialist, who came to the house with a mister. She wasn't sure exactly what he did, but the plants were alive, so he was doing his job. Her husband used him to care for the restaurant plants, so it was all write-off-able, and she didn't have to feel any guilt over it. Plus, Arturo was *lovely* and trying to bring family over from El Salvador (or was it Honduras?), and so she was happy to help support him.

Seraphina laid out her sound-bath instruments—a gong, cymbals, bowls, drums, some kind of guitar . . . an instrumental arsenal.

When everyone had sat down—on the couch, in the chairs, on the upholstered love seat, some on the white shag rug—women were still chatting, chortling, giggling, gasping, and gossiping.

Seraphina closed her eyes and sat on the hardwood floor Indian-style. (Could one still use that expression? Was it called something else now? Who would Milly even ask?)

Milly realized that Seraphina was waiting for them all to be quiet and was too enlightened (or passive-aggressive) to shush them herself, so Milly, still standing by the entrance of the living room, started calming down the group.

"SHHHHHHHHHHHH."

Milly moved toward the sectional and squeezed in next to Eva, who sat next to her wife on the other side.

"SHHHHHHHHHHHH."

Quieter now . . .

"It's so quiet!" loud-whispered Dawn to *anyone within earshot.*

"SHHHHHHHHHHHHHHH."

Silence. Finally.

Milly closed her eyes and settled in. She listened to Seraphina's sounds and inhaled deeply: she heard the rain on the limestone, the droplets falling into the saltwater pool, the crackle of the wood-burning fireplace. She breathed in the scent of designer candles; the crisp, cool breeze from the slightly ajar glass pocket doors.

The cold air felt good on the beads of sweat forming on her nose. She scrunched it, wiping at it with her index finger, the back of her hand brushing Eva's shoulder as she did. They both opened an eye, smiling at one another.

That was all Milly needed to make her feel better.

"OOOOOOOOOOOOMMMMMMMM."

The sound bath had started.

"Close your eyes," Seraphina said, "and come with me on a sensory journey."

Milly closed her eyes, then opened one to make sure everyone else was closing theirs. When she was satisfied that everyone's eyes were closed, she closed her own and settled into the couch, even though she was on the edge, so one of her toned butt cheeks hung off the tiniest bit. She inched closer toward Eva, and in so doing, their hips touched.

"Awahwaheahahwehaah," Seraphina wailed as Milly's body burned with heat and longing.

When Milly had first met Eva years earlier, it was like Eva's eyes had burrowed inside Milly's, traveling through her body, all the way down to her gut like a really expensive, totally comprehensive probiotic (but, like, a sexy one). That was not the best analogy, but really, Milly didn't know how else to describe the immersive power of her evolving feelings for Eva, the feeling of physical transformation throughout her body when this woman looked at her. When their eyes met in the school office, Milly felt it everywhere; she felt it in places of her body she didn't even know she could feel things. She had just recently learned about her pelvic floor in Pilates. She definitely felt it there too. Wherever that was. Milly never imagined her feelings for Eva would be reciprocated, but she'd started fantasizing about it constantly.

Milly didn't think of herself as a lesbian. Not that there was anything wrong with that, of course. Some of her best friends were lesbians. Well, maybe not *best* friends, but she had some *close* lesbian friends for sure.

When she was pregnant with her first child, she'd started watching *The L Word*, and the show awakened something in her. Maybe it was just all the extra hormones coursing through her body at the time, but she was turned on in a way she had never been before.

Suddenly, she wanted to have sex . . . all the time . . . but she didn't want to have sex with her husband. He was so busy and stressed over construction on the two new restaurants, anyway. And she didn't feel sexy; she felt puffy and nauseated and moody. She just wanted to feel *good*, to feel not puffy and not moody and not like a human incubator (even though she and her husband had been through six rounds of IVF to get pregnant the first time, so she truly felt blessed).

In fact, she worried, after having six miscarriages, several "procedures" done to her uterus, and multiple egg retrievals and implantations . . . that all the masturbating she was doing (and subsequent multiple orgasms . . . like, earth-shattering orgasms, one after another after another . . . while watching *The L Word* . . . the original one . . . not the spin-off or the documentary) could cause another miscarriage. She wanted to ask her doctor, but she'd never been a woman who was comfortable talking about masturbation, even with her therapist.

Milly knew there was a smugness to Eva. But also an overwhelming insecurity that presented as defensiveness and reactivity when confronted by angry parents who felt their child's teacher wasn't supportive enough or wasn't adhering to their child's various neurodiverse accommodations, or worse, who took issue with the expensive hot-lunch program that offered neither Glatt kosher nor organic nor nut-free nor dairy-free nor gluten-free options.

It all started pretty late in the pandemic, after vaccines had come out, and people were a little less freaked out about catching COVID. Still, when Eva came down with it, Milly insisted she isolate and convalesce in their designer Murphy bed in their detached, newly renovated (but unpermitted . . . SHHHHH!) guesthouse. The first night Eva was there, Milly brought her a meal—chicken noodle soup and a fresh-baked cookie—served on a tray with a crisp linen napkin, her mother-in-law's china, her grandmother's bequeathed silver, and a rose cut from her garden in a Christofle bud vase she had registered for when she'd gotten engaged to her husband.

Anything for Eva.

What no one knew—or ever would or could know—was that when Milly retrieved the remains of Eva's meal, she lapped up the last sips of Eva's soup from her mother-in-law's china, slurping up backwashed COVID-y broth and two remaining wet noodles. She used her index finger to smash any remaining cookie crumbs until they stuck enough to make it from the plate into her mouth, and she rubbed her fingertip on her top gum like it was cocaine (which she never tried because she knew she'd like it too much). She drank the last bits of herbal tea left in the vintage teacup.

Then she licked the tray from top to bottom.

She wasn't taking any chances.

Two days later, Milly tested positive for COVID.

Years before, after having a hell of a time trying to get pregnant, Milly got a positive pregnancy test. This positive COVID test felt just like that: riddled with anticipation; then relief, excitement, terror, and . . . hope.

So Milly moved into the detached, unpermitted guesthouse with Eva, where ostensibly the two female pals would convalesce together.

Sure, it was a bit awkward at first. They joked about being roommates—Schlemiel and Schlimazel, Thelma and Louise, Kate and Allie—and they played endless games of Rummikub together on the queen-size Murphy bed where Eva was sleeping. That first night, Milly slept on the air mattress next to Eva, and she lay on her side for hours, just watching Eva sleep. When Eva snored softly, it only endeared her more to Milly.

It was in the throes of a heated game of Rummikub, both of them sitting on the unmade Murphy bed, that Milly's manicured, moisturized hand collided with Eva's. They looked up at each other over their tiles, and Milly thought, in that moment, she had never seen a human as beautiful, as sexy, as interesting, as smart, as strong, as inhalable as Eva was.

Sure, Eva's nose was red from blowing it for three days and her voice was still nasally. Milly had a cough and a tickle in her throat, but the tickle between her legs was stronger and took over. The way that Eva looked at her . . . Could she have feelings for Milly too?

Milly still couldn't believe what she'd done next: she leaned forward, kissing Eva lightly on the lips.

Eva's lips were *so soft*. Softer even than she had imagined they would be. And she had imagined it a lot. But there was one problem: Eva didn't kiss her back.

Milly sat back, terrified. Eva stared at her, expressionless. What had Milly done? She had crossed a line. Many lines. They were both married. They were both women. Eva was the principal of her child's school. They were isolating together in her detached, unpermitted guesthouse, with a communicable virus. Milly knew she had gone too far. She had made a terrible mistake. How could she do something so stupid, so reckless . . .

"I'm so sorry," Milly said. "I don't . . . It must be the fever—"

Eva leaned forward, her face inscrutable. Milly hung her head, embarrassed, ashamed, shocked, and furious with herself. She'd ruined everything!

Eva put her hand under Milly's chin, raising her face up to hers. Her eyes hesitantly made contact with Eva's. Before she could apologize again, Eva leaned over and kissed Milly . . .

Milly couldn't believe it—was this a dream? But even in her dreams, it didn't feel this good, Eva's cheek as soft as a ripe peach, a welcome contrast to her husband's stubble, which, if she was comparing both their faces to fruit, was more like a kiwi.

Milly didn't know where to put her hands . . . or anything else. She had never kissed another woman before. Sure, she'd seen *The L Word*, all the seasons, multiple times, but she didn't know what to do. She went to put her arms around Eva, but Eva lightly pushed her back down, and they continued kissing, faster, harder, deeper. It was better, sweeter, softer, sexier, more thrilling than any kiss before. Eva put her hand down Milly's cashmere athleisure pants, and Milly gasped—

"AWOOOOOOOOO," howled Seraphina as Milly was jolted out of her memory and back into the reality of the party-book party sound bath.

She had to get her bearings and catch her breath. Meanwhile, Eva was sitting beside her now, and Milly was so turned on just by her proximity that she didn't know what to do with herself.

As Seraphina played various instruments and the rain poured outside, Milly felt Eva lean closer to her. Just the slightest tilt. But that was all Milly needed to feel heat throughout her entire body. No, it was more than heat. It was an electric shock. It was a shock so intense she worried her hair might stand on end like a character in one of her son's graphic novels.

Fuck, how she wanted to fuck Eva right then. But she couldn't. Obviously. So she closed her eyes and went back to the memory of how their relationship began.

Eva had used Milly's positive COVID test results to stay shacked up in the detached guesthouse with her for another five days. They joked it was their "COVID and chill." Eva could be really funny. For those moms who didn't think she had a sense of humor, they just didn't know her. Milly marveled at how no one recognized just how wonderful Eva could be. No one knew her as well or appreciated her as much as Milly did. Certainly Mags did not.

It had been more than a year since their "COVID and chill," but Milly still went into her guesthouse some days, releasing the blond-wood Murphy bed from the wall so she could smell Eva, or at least try to re-create the feeling she'd had over those few sex-filled days.

Before Milly had met Eva, nothing seemed to bring her more joy or fulfillment than sample sales. Sure, she had two children and she loved them. But she loved her kids in a different way than she loved sample sales. The sales—and her spoils from them—were all hers. Getting something at more than 60 percent off gave her a better high than a bottle of Sancerre on an empty stomach or the most expensive vape pen. Sample-sale shopping was her drug of choice, her rush, and she took it very seriously.

Milly's mind would sometimes wander in ecstasy to how she'd bought her favorite brightly colored Natalie Martin caftan at a sample sale for 70 percent off, at a friend of a friend of a friend's English Tudor manse in Hancock Park.

She had waited in the driveway with a line of other women eager to buy $450 caftans and accessories for a fraction of their retail price. The women stood in full sun (most wore oversize brimmed hats, and those who didn't shared their sunscreen, along with their Beverly Hills dermatologists' direct cell phone numbers, because . . . that's how you lean in, ladies).

That was a start, at least. Milly had been waiting in the line for almost forty-five minutes when three women wearing large sunglasses just walked past it and through the front door. Mags, Eva's wife, was one of them. Milly seethed. Not leaning in! She didn't realize she was clenching her fists until she felt the pinch of her freshly manicured nails piercing the palms of her hands. It was just clear polish, but now she'd have blood under her nails and the manicure was basically ruined. Ugh.

She tried to breathe deeply like she'd learned to do in the Introduction to Transcendental Meditation class she'd won at the school raffle two years before. She kept thinking she'd go back to it, but then . . . life got in the way, and just . . . who had time for meditation, anyway? Also, she forgot her mantra. She blamed it on mom brain, but if she was being honest, meditation bored her.

Once she finally gained entrance into the drought-friendly, child-friendly, chic-friendly backyard (the best artificial turf, succulents, and

Mexican beach pebble), Milly thought about how ironic it was that the Mexican beach pebble was the most expensive of the landscaping pebbles. And the Mexican workers—the ones who actually carried and scattered the huge bags of rocks—probably got paid less per hour than the cost of a handful of these beach pebbles from their own country. This depressed Milly. Why was the world so unfair and cruel? She was always kind to everyone, and made a mental note to herself to be super-kind to her gardener that week, maybe slip him extra money.

Milly was a firm believer in karma. She didn't really buy into reincarnation, but she thought if it *was* a thing, she really hoped she would *not* come back as a migrant worker.

Anyway, she didn't want to think of any of that, as she was finally in the backyard among the racks of clothes being ravaged, and every moment spent thinking of other people's misfortunes or "the greater good" or whatever was a missed opportunity to acquire a piece she would wear and dine out on for years before selling it for store credit to the RealReal.

After grabbing piles of dresses in her arms, she took her spoils inside the dark-wood manse, where thirty women were changing in the bright living room in front of original floor-to-ceiling single-paned windows, stripping down unselfconsciously like Milly's mother and grandmother used to do when she was a child and they would take her to Loehmann's. But this was not Loehmann's. No, Loehmann's was a common denominator. There, Milly saw naked women of all colors, shapes, and sizes. This sample sale in a posh home in Hancock Park was, for the most part, a white-lady party, and almost everyone was in the market for size small.

Milly tried not to make eye contact with anyone. She wasn't there to socialize. Women, total strangers, asked advice from each other, gave compliments, or scrunched their noses and questioned:

"But do you need it?"

A-, B-, C-, and D-list actresses, some of whom could easily get one of these dresses for free for just an Insta post or a TikTok video, stood in the buff, trying not to elbow the stranger to their right, as they modeled twelve versions of the same dress in different patterns and fabrics. Like Milly, these women came to sample sales for sport as much as anything else.

Women wearing only billowy silk blouses and designer thongs ran in and out of the house to the racks in the backyard to find another size before someone else could take it. Milly had always been modest about changing in front of other women. Her excitement about 70 percent off trumped her modesty, but she still tried everything on over her James Perse tank top (also bought at a sample sale). If someone had told her that she would go from this kind of modesty around other women to having another woman's mouth and fingers inside her (and hers inside another woman), well, she would have laughed out loud. She wasn't laughing now.

Because then she'd met Eva, and nothing about Milly—about her life, her values, her priorities, her desires—had been the same since. Outwardly, of course, everything was the same; it had to be that way. But inwardly, she had changed. Milly was supposed to be the sweet, heterosexual Mother of Dragons. But now Milly would take the long, silk caftan she'd fought for at that sample sale, and she would throw it over her shoulder so she could look down and see Eva's beautiful face between her legs.

She thought about how she would give up ever going to any sample sale ever again if it meant getting to spend the rest of her life with Eva.

And yet, no one could ever know about their relationship. They were both married. They had kids in the same school! Eva was the fucking principal.

Milly was fucking the fucking principal.

She would be lying if she said that it didn't make her feel special. It had been a long time since Milly felt special. But no, it would always have to be a secret. It would be a scandal if anyone knew. It would blow up a lot of innocent lives. She was *not* a homewrecker, and she did not want to wreck anyone else's home or family or marriage or anything, ever.

No one could ever know. Ever. Never. Ever.

Never.

Ever.

That aspect of it made her really depressed when she actually thought about it. So she actively tried not to think about her future with or without Eva. But in this moment, they were together. Or at least, they were sitting together. She could feel Eva next to her, the heat rising between them. To Milly, it felt like they were the only two people in the world. Until she reminded herself that Eva's wife was on the other side of her. And they were in a room full of women at a school-sanctioned event. She had to get a hold of herself.

The plan had originally been for Eva to stay at Milly's house after the sound-bath party. Milly's husband would be working late at the restaurant and the kids would be asleep, so she and Eva could "work on the fundraising plan." Of course, she would actually do the fundraising plan on her own during the day when the kids were at school, after she did the Peloton and took their labradoodle for a walk and masturbated with Goop's latest vibrator, thinking about Eva and how much of a fucking boss she was.

She had been eagerly anticipating her time alone with Eva that night. She had been planning on it, fantasizing about it, since they hadn't been able to find a way to meet in private for two weeks. So that was why it was a gut punch for Milly when Mags showed up at the sound-bath party with Eva. In that moment, Milly knew Eva would not be hers that night, and she was surprised by how hurt and disappointed and angry she felt.

Maybe they would FaceTime later and Eva could talk Milly through how she would go down on her as Milly masturbated to her slow, descriptive narration. Eva was really good at that. But it wasn't the same as actually being together—Eva's tongue caressing hers; her hand between Milly's legs, touching her in ways she didn't even know how to touch herself to make herself feel that fucking euphoric.

You know what word Middle-Aged Moms don't use often to describe how they feel? *Euphoric.* But Milly felt euphoric when she was with Eva, and that was why she couldn't—wouldn't—stop.

Maybe Eva would stay late with her at school this week. It wouldn't be the first time they fucked in Eva's office—on the desk, on the couch, on the floor—and she always hoped it wouldn't be the last. Her husband would be at one or all the restaurants and bars until two every night. He was training a new hostess at his flagship restaurant this week. The last one had left him for a job at Spago, which he took personally, but Milly assured him it was her loss because "Wolfgang Puck is so nineties."

What did Milly really think? She thought that Wolfgang Puck was a timeless fucking genius. But her husband didn't need to know that. He didn't need to know a lot of things. Most importantly, he didn't need to know what Milly was just starting to realize: that her relationship with Eva had become much more than sexual. Milly was in love with Eva.

GONG!

The deep sound of the gong brought Milly back from her musings. She refocused and tried to let the sound bath and the warmth of Eva's body wash over her.

Jillian

Jillian, nursing her fifth glass of wine, slipped into the already-started sound bath, sitting quietly on the white shag in Milly's living room. She was late because she'd had to down her fourth glass quickly and pour another one (to the brim!) without anyone seeing. She needed it after what had happened that afternoon. She was still in shock. But she knew that what had happened didn't happen in a vacuum. It didn't happen out of nowhere. She had to think about what had led her there . . . here . . . to this point . . . What *drove her to do what she had done.*

The last few months had been a real bear for her, and her husband's family in particular. Her husband's parents, who had immigrated to the United States in the last ten years, had both died within three months of each other. Jillian had been holding her father-in-law's hand when he took his last breath. At that moment, her husband was standing on a rickety wooden chair behind her, fiddling with a broken window shade in the broom closet of a room in a shitty skilled-nursing facility (where the nurses were not terribly skilled).

Jillian watched her father-in-law with compassion, terror, regret, guilt, sadness, and fascination. Not necessarily in that order. She had never seen anyone die before, let alone held someone's hand as they passed. She counted the beats between his slowing breaths as they became fewer and farther between. It was all much quieter, slower, less dramatic than she'd imagined death would be. But she would never forget that lightness she felt in the room after he took his last breath. It was an energy shift. But it was so slight that if you blinked, you might have missed it. A vibrant, full life . . . just . . . over. Poof. Gone.

She stared at him . . . What was once a loving, living, breathing, animated man was now just a shell.

Game-fucking-over.

Jillian waited until her husband came down from standing on the unbalanced chair and futzing with the shades "so that the sun won't wake my dad up in the morning" to tell him that no morning sun, no light, no frothy cappuccino, no fresh-baked bread, no smelling salts, no warm hugs from loving grandchildren, no nothing was going to wake his father ever again.

His father was dead.

Jillian's husband hadn't believed it. His father "wasn't supposed to die tonight," he said. And he certainly didn't want Jillian to be there when it happened. She knew he didn't think she could handle something like that.

Jillian took a step back, away from the fresh corpse. It's true this was not something she was emotionally prepared for that day. Or any day. Who is? Maybe a coroner? Anyway, it probably didn't help that she had taken an Adderall that morning. She was on deadline for something she was writing, and also she liked to try all the pills she was hawking to other moms so she could speak to how they might make them feel. If she was going to be a drug dealer, she was going to be a good one. She was, after all, an Ivy League perfectionist.

Jillian knew her husband would worry about her, her struggles with depression and anxiety . . . and how this, holding his father's hand as he died in front of her, might make her spiral. Little did he know or realize, that for all her issues, for all her privileged white-woman disorders, for all her arguably self-imposed trauma, she was resilient as fuck. She was strong. She was a survivor. She forgot that sometimes, but in this moment, she remembered it. And she felt relief.

Of course, that might have been the Adderall.

She wasn't sure if she didn't cry because she was in shock or because of the horse pill of Zoloft she took every day. Either way, she didn't cry a single tear as she drove home, alone, letting her husband deal with the paperwork and the cremation details and his father's body.

She had suggested they could get a discount from the crematorium since they had just paid for her mother-in-law's cremation a few months before, but apparently "it didn't work that way."

Assholes.

She'd been raised on the saying *If you don't ask, you don't get.* Kind of like when she would go to hotels . . . back when they could afford to go to hotels . . . and she would check in by saying (*very nicely and with a smile*), "Why don't you just give me the room you're going to give me three rooms from now?"

After her father-in-law died, she had to pick up their kids, who were swimming at a neighbor's house. Jillian and her husband couldn't afford a pool, though they often talked about building one someday. *Someday.* Jillian thought about how there were a lot of "somedays" in her marriage.

A pool? Someday.

A job? Someday.

Sex? Someday.

Being able to pay for private school instead of her parents paying for it? Someday.

Just that morning, she had asked her parents for more financial help—a "bridge loan," if you will. And they had said no. They had never told her no before this. They suggested she could sell their house.

And go where?

Jillian was spinning.

The clang of cymbals jolted Jillian out of her musing. She opened an eye. The sound-bath-leader woman caught her peeking, and she quickly closed it.

Looking back now, from her seat on an imported designer shag carpet at a sound-bath party-book party, her legs tucked underneath her, it should have been no surprise to Jillian or anyone what happened with Flynn, her daughter's new, controversial, oft-maligned, and wildly inexperienced teacher.

She had been about to check out that afternoon at Trader Joe's (with eight boxes of soup dumplings, even though the sign clearly said the limit on soup dumplings was five) when she remembered to get those mini cones her kids loved (and to be fair, she loved them too—they were the perfect size . . . even if "the perfect size" meant she ended up eating three or more of them at a time).

As she reached into the freezer to grab the last box of vanilla mini cones, she couldn't help but notice the shadow of a man bun. In West Hollywood, this was a decidedly ubiquitous shadow, but when she looked up, she locked eyes with Flynn, her daughter's teacher whom she had been reviling and trying to get fired by signing multiple petitions to that effect.

"Are those good?" he asked.

"I don't know. I don't eat them. They're for the kids."

Lies.

"You're, ummm—"

"Jillian."

"Right! I'm—"

"Flynn. Yes, I know."

"Listen, we kind of got off on the wrong foot . . . I know that you feel I'm not qualified and I don't know how to write recommendations, but—"

"I don't think this is the time or the place."

"It's as good as any."

"We're in Frozen Foods."

"Would you rather talk in Nuts?"

"Was that a joke?"

"If you have to ask, it's not a good one."

Jillian smiled. Why was she smiling? She hated this guy!

"Why do you hate me?" he asked.

"I don't 'hate' you. In fact, we don't use the *H* word in our house."

"Interesting."

"What does that mean?"

"It's just that your daughter uses the word *hate* quite often."

Jillian made a mental note to reiterate the *H*-word rule when she got home.

"Here's the thing, Flynn: We're just trying to get our daughter into middle school . . . and you haven't written recommendations before, and you don't know our daughter or our family or anything about the schools to which we're applying, and you don't really have any teaching experience, and I've heard that you play sitcom episodes for them during school hours, and Eva doesn't like me, so . . . I just don't want my daughter to suffer because of . . . me. And society at large. But mostly . . . me. And you."

"So why don't I get to know you?"

"To know me is not necessarily to love me," said Jillian.

"HUH, HUH, HUH—from your gut!" boomed Seraphina.

Jillian opened her eyes to see the women around her earnestly trying to make sounds from their "gut." Jillian did not want to make sounds from her gut. She needed to replay what had happened with Flynn.

After she'd checked out at Trader Joe's, Flynn offered to help Jillian with her bags, but she insisted she was fine . . . until a dozen eggs spilled out of her reusable grocery bag and she started to cry uncontrollably (peri-fucking-menopause), which made her even angrier with herself and the situation (more peri-fucking-menopause).

"Let me help you," he said.

"No!"

She started to clean it up as Flynn walked away.

Seriously? She couldn't believe he just left!

"Here," he said, now kneeling beside her with a roll of paper towels he had pulled out of thin air like a paper-product wizard. He wiped up the mess. "Just a few cracked eggs. All okay."

Jillian knew it was just a tiny thing, a kind gesture. But it had felt important, meaningful. Why? Because she had to make everything okay for everyone all the time. It was exhausting. She was so accustomed to it she hadn't even realized it until this moment. She tried to shake it off, but the reality was that it had been so long since a man had made something, anything, okay for her.

She had married someone who was the opposite of her father, on purpose. What she didn't realize was that, by marrying the opposite of her father, who was a successful and controlling businessman, she would have to become her father. Or at least, a version of him. Because you can't have two dreamers in a marriage . . . especially not in Hollywood. Someone has to have a real job to refinance the mortgage . . . and Jillian hated that that person had become her. It wasn't supposed to be her.

But here she was. The breadwinner of the family, a semisuccessful writer who got paid to write things that never actually got made, an Adderall pusher, a mom, a wife, and a deeply unhappy woman who was crushed under her mental load, had become increasingly terrible at self-care, and was definitely going through perimenopause, which was her new favorite topic of conversation and also favorite podcast subject.

She was parked on P2 of the garage at Trader Joe's—not because there weren't spots on P1, but because she didn't want to see anyone and she preferred *not* parking next to another car since, well, LA drivers were assholes.

The shopping cart locked halfway to the car, and Flynn insisted on carrying her bags. With every nice thing he did, the harder it became for Jillian to hate him or want to work toward getting him fired. He was so much nicer and more genuine than she wanted him to be so she could continue to villainize him. As he put her groceries in her minivan, he hit his head on the trunk lid.

"Are you okay? I'm sorry. I think I have a first aid thing in my car—"

"It's fine. I'm okay."

"Are you sure?"

"Sure I'm sure."

"Okay, well . . . Thank you. For your help. Can I give you a ride to your car? It's the least I can do now that you have a concussion."

"It's okay. I biked here."

"How about a ride to your bike?"

"Sure."

He got in the passenger seat as she got in the driver's seat.

"This is nice."

Jillian nodded. How was she supposed to respond to that?

"It's . . . how the car came. I got a deal on the lease. I negotiate our leases, usually, because my husband . . . Well, whatever."

Flynn nodded.

"No money down, which is, y'know, great. So. Yeah . . ." Jillian continued.

"I don't have a car."

"In LA? How is that possible?"

"I bike. I Uber. Bus. I mooch rides from friends. I do Zipcars sometimes."

"Isn't that annoying? Like, having to figure out how you're going to get places?"

"Not really. I think of it as kind of an adventure . . . or like a big escape room."

"Oh. I'm claustrophobic, so . . . no escape rooms for me."

"Are you, though? Claustrophobic?"

"I am."

"Or is that just what you tell yourself?"

"No, I'm definitely claustrophobic."

"I bet you're not. Not really."

"Okay. But I am."

Now Jillian was annoyed. How the fuck would he know whether she was actually claustrophobic or not? She'd once tried to have her eyelashes tinted, not realizing she would need to keep her eyes closed for ten minutes without opening them. She'd made it about fourteen seconds before shrieking and opening her eyes while the dye was still on, so the dye ran down her face and hands and everything burned and all the technicians scrambled to wash out her eyes. She wrote a scathing Yelp review but later deleted it after her therapist had helped her realize that they hadn't done anything wrong.

She turned on the ignition to the car, and Aimee Mann was singing "Save Me," because Jillian often sat in the car to cry and that was a good song for it. Jillian turned to Flynn.

"I'm sorry."

"Why? I love Aimee Mann."

"I meant . . . I'm sorry . . . for how I've acted. Not giving you a chance as a teacher. I just feel so much pressure. With admissions and everything else. Honestly, sometimes I don't even recognize myself anymore."

"Hey," he said, "it's okay. I see you." He put his hand on hers, which was on her knee. He squeezed it. Jillian couldn't help but feel something . . . something she hadn't felt in so long . . . Could it be longing? For her daughter's annoying teacher? Absolutely not.

Then she started to cry. Again.

"Oh my God . . . this is so embarrassing. I don't know what's wrong with me. Probably a perimenopause thing—"

"I don't think anything's wrong with you. What do you mean by 'peri'?"

Through tears, she was happy to explain and educate. "It's like premenopause . . . It's what comes before . . . If you're really interested, there are a lot of podcasts you could listen to—"

"Maybe take some breaths? Like this." Flynn breathed in through his nose and exhaled through his mouth. "I do this with the kids in class. Try it with me," he said.

Jillian shook her head, wiped her eyes, and took a few deep breaths with Flynn.

"You feel better, right?"

"Not really."

"You want to fuck?" he asked.

Wait. What?

She studied his expression. She looked around for the *Candid Camera* crew.

She had never cheated on her husband. She had never fucked in a car—or anywhere interesting, for that matter. Once, when she was seventeen, a guy went down on her on the beach. And her takeaway was that it was . . . sandy. In college, she had sex with a Spanish exchange student in her closet on the linoleum floor. Looking back, it was unclear why the closet, why the floor, and it wasn't terribly comfortable, nor was it kinky or interesting. But he'd had a great accent. That part she remembered.

This, on the other hand, in her sensible minivan on P2 of the TJs parking garage in West Hollywood, was definitely . . . interesting. Flynn used the bottom of his own shirt to wipe away a tear from her face, and in so doing exposed his abs, which, unlike her husband's dad-bod abs, were pretty fucking ripped.

She wasn't usually someone who cared about that stuff—for her own body, she did, of course, but she never needed to date guys with crazy-cut bodies. Flynn's body was . . . particularly interesting to her, though . . . and she wanted to know more about it. To see more. To feel more. Or some. Or any.

But that was crazy! She was married. If she was going to cheat, it should be with someone who could take her on a yacht in the south of France and deal with refinancing mortgages. She had never cheated on anyone or anything before. One could call Jillian a lot of things. *Cheater* was not one of them. Not until today, at least. Of course, she hadn't done anything wrong. Yet.

Jillian was uncharacteristically at a loss for words.

On one hand, she knew she should say, *"How dare you? I am a married woman! I am a good twenty years older than you are! Like, I became legal to drink the year you were born, and how fucked up is that? Also, you are my daughter's teacher! Also, how dare you?"*

And on the other hand, she wanted to say, *"Thank you."*

Just *thank you.* Thank you for your interest. Thank you for your service. Thank you for your attention. Thank you for seeing me as something other than a mother and a wife. Thank you, thank you, thank you. Thank you, you weirdly hot man-child with a messy man bun and abs of steel.

Truly, Jillian was hard pressed to remember the last time someone who wasn't her husband had looked twice at her, let alone asked her to "fuck."

"Are you serious?" she asked. "About the . . . fucking?"

He shrugged.

"That is *so nice.* Really. I mean, maybe I should be offended . . . but I'm not. I'm flattered. But I don't . . . yeah, I don't do that and I don't think so. I'm married. And you're my daughter's teacher. And . . . the ice-cream cones . . . they're pretty small . . . They're probably melting."

Flynn shrugged again.

"K," he said.

"'K'?"

"Hmm?"

There were so many things she could have done. She could have told him to get out of the car angrily (the "How dare you" option). She could have asked him to please get out of the car nicely (the "I'm flattered, but . . ." option).

Instead, she asked, out of genuine curiosity, "Do you . . . want to . . . fuck *me?"*

It felt like an out-of-body experience just having the conversation, saying these words, and it felt wrong. But also exciting. Her entire everything was tingling. She hadn't felt so alive in years. Decades! What was this feeling?

"I wouldn't ask if I didn't want to."

"Really? I mean . . . really?"

"You're hot. I noticed you at Back to School Night."

"You did?"

"Yeah."

"I should tell you, I've signed petitions to have you fired."

"I heard one of those was going around."

"There's more than one."

"Oh."

"You're not upset?"

"You're advocating for your kid. My mom did the same for me growing up. Mama bears protect their young. Respect."

"Right. Mama bears."

"I'm just drawn to you. You're giving off a vibe. It's awesome. Don't you feel it?"

"Do you even know my name—"

"Yes, you just told me. You're . . . the mom of—"

"You don't remember my daughter's name either."

"I'm not great with names. Never have been. Faces! Faces, I don't forget. I have a friend and he says he has that face-blindness thing—you know, the thing where he can barely recognize his own mother, let alone someone he only met once. But I don't know . . . I think maybe he just smokes too much weed."

"Jillian."

He stared at her blankly.

"Is my name."

"Oh, right. Jillian. That's a nice name."

"Thank you."

"So . . ."

"So . . ."

"You want to fuck, *Jillian*?"

They looked at each other and both broke into a smile. She started laughing . . . a little at first, and then that uncontrollable laugh she used to get with her friends at summer camp, when she was sure she couldn't stop and she may very well pee in her pants and she didn't even remember what she was laughing about anymore. Tears flowed from her eyes. And soon she wasn't sure if she was laughing or crying or both.

Flynn seemed remarkably unfazed. Could this man be the perimenopause whisperer she hadn't known she needed?

She finally got her laughter under control. She dabbed her eyes, wiped her nose, and took a deep breath.

"You feel better?" he asked.

Jillian nodded, but when she looked at Flynn, she started laughing again. "I don't know what's wrong with me."

"I think you just needed a good laugh. And maybe a good fuck too."

"I don't think us . . . having sex . . . is appropriate, Flynn, but I am flattered. Really flattered. And also horrified. And I can't believe we're having this conversation."

And then the Spice Girls came on.

"Sorry, it's nineties music . . . I like to listen to it. Nostalgia, you know?"

Jillian tried to forward to the next track.

"I like oldies."

"Nineties are not *oldies*."

"Really?"

"No. Doo-wop is oldies. Nineties is . . . my college years."

"Doo-wop?"

"Yeah, you know, like, *bah didi bah did dang di dang dang dooodoo—*"

Flynn put his hand on her knee again. She stopped doo-wopping. They looked at each other.

Jesus-fucking-Christ.

Jillian exhaled, exasperated . . . and also completely turned on.

She wondered if she had already transgressed by just having the conversation without kicking him out of the car and calling her husband.

"Can I put my hand between your legs?" he asked.

She didn't answer. She maybe nodded, but she wasn't sure. She was a bit paralyzed. He started to put his hand down her pants, but the drawstring on her five-year-old Vuoris (they last forever!) was double-knotted. He leaned over and used his teeth to open the knot on her sweats—the sweats she'd jokingly called her "I give up" pants.

She thought, in that moment, she would have to rebrand them to her "I give *it* up" pants. She laughed to herself. Humor was literally all she had left. Humor and her daughter's teacher's hand down her pants.

Jillian's heart quickened as Flynn's hand moved between her legs. She couldn't undo this, she thought. What was she doing? Wait, she deserved this, for fuck's sake. Her husband was a disappointment. And fuck, this felt good, even though she knew it was awful and wrong. Yes, she'd married her husband for better or for worse but—

"You're so wet," Flynn purred in her ear.

"I am?!"

It had been a long time since that had happened and frankly, she didn't think she was capable of it anymore. She felt . . . optimistic. Among other things. She felt so much! It felt so good to feel something, anything, outside of anxiety and anger and disappointment and responsibility.

He was breathing into her ear as his hand moved faster.

Jillian climbed on top of Flynn so she was straddled over his lap in the passenger seat. She kissed him. She hadn't kissed anyone else in almost two decades, and she'd forgotten what it was like to really use her tongue. Somewhere along the way, she and her husband had started using less tongue. Flynn's tongue was a bit slimy and tasted like . . . Was it matcha? Probably. That would be on brand. But she didn't care. They both tried to pull off her pants, but then they got caught on her running shoes, which she had to take off—why was everything in her life double-knotted?!

She was so preoccupied dealing with her double knots that by the time she focused back on Flynn, his pants were unzipped and his cock was out and he was hard as a fucking rock . . . and . . . What the actual fuck?

"Oh," she said.

"What's wrong?"

"I mean . . . everything."

"Do you want to stop?"

"No," she said. There was no turning back now. She hadn't felt this turned on in . . . maybe ever? She felt like an entirely different person: a person who didn't need CBD lube to have hot sex with younger men with man buns in minivans in parking garages.

And by the time Indigo Girls came on, Jillian was riding her daughter's teacher in the passenger seat of her minivan.

So yeah, it wasn't the sexiest soundtrack.

She didn't come. She couldn't. She was too stressed, too in her head. Too guilty. Maybe even too excited. But she pretended to. She had gotten good at that over the years.

"Fuck, Jillian . . ." Flynn gasped as he came inside her. Luckily, she had an IUD and was going through the aforementioned perimenopause, so she didn't have to worry about pregnancy, but, oh shit, what about STDs? Did she need to worry about that now? Ugh.

Were crabs still a thing? That was the last thing she needed. Who knew where this guy had been (aside from West Hollywood Trader Joe's and, of course, her daughter's school)?

"That was . . . awesome."

"Yeah. Wow. Well, I can't undo that," she said, lifting off his lap and pulling her sweats back on as she moved into the driver's seat.

She changed the track from Indigo Girls.

And on came a podcast narrator:

"When you experience vaginal dryness in perimenopause, it usually—"

She quickly went back to the Indigo Girls and turned the volume down.

Who could she even tell about this? She couldn't trust anyone with this secret. She was in a daze. She wanted him out of her car.

"Listen . . . that was a one-off . . . okay? I've never done anything like this and I can't . . . You're my daughter's teacher . . ."

"My lips are sealed."

There was an awkward silence.

"I can just walk to my bike, I guess."

"Sure. That's probably a good idea."

Flynn got out of the car.

"Well, uh, I guess I'll see you at school?"

"Yup! Sounds great!"

"Oh, one more thing . . ." he said, and he leaned in. Jillian leaned toward him, wondering where this was going now. Did he want to go again?

"Your daughter wants to take the classroom pet rats home this weekend. That cool with you?"

"Oh. Um . . . rats . . . yup. Sure. Sounds great."

"Cool, cool. They're really easy to take care of. You'll see. You'll want to keep them."

"I doubt that."

He tapped the door with his palm and closed it. He walked over to his bike and she watched him in the rearview as the Indigo Girls song "Closer to Fine" came on Jillian's car stereo.

Jillian did not feel close to fine.

OMG, what had she done?

She had to find her stupid parking ticket. Fuck. Where had she put it? When she'd entered this parking garage, she was a regular—if frustrated and unhappy—woman who had never cheated on her husband. And now she was leaving (if she could find her fucking ticket!) with another man's cum inside her.

She found her ticket, the gate lifted (silver lining: she made it within the free hour, so she didn't even have to pay), and she drove home in shock.

"Fuck!" Jillian yelled, in tears, as she pounded on the steering wheel. *"Fuuuuuuuuuuuuck!"* And then she started laughing uncontrollably. She was, indeed, losing it.

She had hoped the sound bath would cleanse her, maybe even absolve her of her transgressions in some way, but so far, as the bowls and gongs rang out around her, she could only play the episode back in her mind over and over, wondering if she would—or could—ever feel that passion again.

Heather

Heather's eyes were closed during the sound bath. But she wasn't moaning or otherwise participating in the bizarrely cacophonous event that in no way reminded her of a "bath" of any kind. She was not focused on "healing" or "manifesting" or "letting it all out" (ugh). No, she was writing her brief in her head. If only she had her computer there. Either way, she would bill the client for this time.

She was also thinking that if she got home and her son was still up and not showered, she would definitely *not* have sex with her husband.

If her husband hadn't already taken the dog out by the time she got there, she would definitely *not* have sex with him.

The reality was, she would probably not have sex with him anyway, but it felt good to put conditions on it. As if she were leaving the door open to it, like a "good" wife should.

Heather knew she was not a "good" wife. Whatever that meant.

A "good" wife didn't belittle her husband in front of their children and other couples. A "good" wife wouldn't let their baby die within hours of being born. She knew, logically, the second one wasn't her fault. It didn't matter; she would always feel that guilt, the guilt that somehow it was because of her that he'd died. That somehow, some way, it was her fault, physiologically. Or that she'd done something to deserve it. And for her wrongs, an innocent baby had suffered—their innocent baby.

Perhaps that was the kind of thinking, years before, that had gotten her into the mess with Dawn's husband in the first place. Since he was one of the partners in her law firm then, everyone answered to him. They all knew he was a douche, but he was a machine and uniquely good at his job, and for that, Heather respected him. As a lawyer, Heather always weighed competency higher than manners or likability. She expected people to do the same with her.

After the death of her first child, HR had told her she could take her maternity leave to convalesce and mourn. But she knew that wouldn't bring her son back. It wouldn't change what had happened. It would just give her more time to dwell on the trauma. More time to stare at a baby-less nursery, to fixate on the empty crib and the designer nursing glider meant for a baby who no longer existed. It would give her more time to gaze at the unused changing table with its fresh box of wipes, which would dry up because no one would use them.

No, thank you. No, staying home was the last thing she needed.

And so she donated most of what was in her nursery to a local charity run by benevolent socialite moms who were known for, among other more important things, throwing the best charity ball in Los Angeles. She was back to work in less than a week after the birth and death of her first child.

And it totally freaked out everyone at her firm.

She was still bleeding, still wearing thick pads; she still looked pregnant, and because she hadn't gotten the shot they'd offered her in the hospital, her milk had come in, so she was using different smelly lotions and a compression bra to stop it. She squeezed her nipples in the shower, and her engorged breasts sprayed milk that would never help a small human—her small human—grow. There she was, alone, in the shower, spraying milk into the ether, watching as it circled and literally disappeared down the drain.

Well.

It simply wasn't efficient or beneficial for her to feel sorry for herself. It was better to get back to work. Work was tangible. Making money was tangible. That, she could do. That, she had control over. But most people at the office wouldn't look her in the eye . . . or worse, they would look at her with pity. No one knew what to say. She wasn't one for small chat on a good day, let alone these days. And she *hated* being pitied.

That was why she was grateful when Dawn's husband approached her as she refilled her water bottle in the firm's kitchen and immediately moved into a legal discussion, dumping multiple new cases and clients on her. She was grateful for his professionalism, for his lack of sentimentalism. She was grateful he saw her value as legal counsel rather than her failure as a woman who could grow and deliver a healthy baby.

From that point on, she preferred to work with Dawn's husband over any other partners for exactly that reason. In his own weird way, he "got" Heather. It may not have been that he understood her, but he was able to give her exactly what she needed, when she needed it.

They didn't make small talk when they worked together. They didn't ask about each other's lives. They didn't tell jokes or offer to get each other coffee. They didn't refer to each other as their "work husband" and "work wife." There weren't niceties or bullshit. They just *worked*. They had the same cutthroat way of coping with and relating to others. Neither of them was well liked around the office. Neither of them cared. They were effective. They didn't canoodle or gossip or share anything outside of a Google Doc; they just got shit done.

And so it went on like that for months. They worked together on important, timely cases and clients and deals. Late nights. Early mornings. Weekends. Emails, texts, phone calls. No banter. No getting to know each other. No memes or GIFs or whatever the fuck people sent each other over text to waste time. They were a phenomenally efficient team.

And then there was the firm retreat to San Diego.

Which they both felt was a waste of time and resources, a distraction from work. They ditched the "How to Combat Prejudice, Bias, and Stereotypes" lecture, choosing to meet in a bar where they could work without distraction. But they also drank, which led to them both getting uncharacteristically wasted.

They didn't laugh or flirt or share personal information, even when drunk. They were serious people doing serious things, after all, and that was what they shared: an intensity, a lack of sensitivity, a professional drive above all else.

But even the most laser-focused professionals have physical needs. And those needs tend to surface more easily when type A workaholics let down their guard and get wasted in the middle of the day on a company retreat.

They had both lost track of how many vodka gimlets they had ordered when Dawn's husband's assistant texted to remind him he was one of the hosts of the firm's dinner that evening, which was starting imminently. The day had gotten away from them.

They split the check and went back to their respective rooms, which were across the hall from each other.

"I'll see you at dinner," she said.

"Yup," he said.

Heather scanned her key card. The lock lit up green and clicked open. She opened the door to her room, but Dawn's husband struggled with his key card, dropping it on the floor.

"You okay?" she asked halfway inside her room.

"Fucking key card. I hate these things."

He held it to the door, but it kept blinking red.

"*Fuck!* Why can't these things ever fucking work?"

A housekeeper down the hall scurried away with her cart as he started kicking the door.

Accustomed to these outbursts from him, Heather said calmly, "Let me try."

He gave her the key card and she tried. The red light came up. Again.

"Fuck!" he yelled. "Hey, you! Miss!" he called out to the housekeeper. But she pretended not to hear him and pushed her cart around the corner and out of sight.

"You can use my room to call down to the front desk," Heather said.

"Fine. Thanks."

He kicked the door one more time for good measure and followed Heather into her hotel room. They stood there awkwardly for a moment.

The phone was on the desk in her room. She walked over and stood in front of it. She looked in the mirror as he came up behind her. She stared straight ahead, connecting with him through the mirror's reflection with her back still to him. Heather watched him as she slowly unbuttoned her shirt, his mouth dropping, and she leaned her hands on the desk.

Heather did not want him in her bed if she could avoid it. She was fine to fuck on the desk or leaning on the desk or whatever proximity to the desk because she had seen an investigative report about the cleanliness (or lack thereof) of bedspreads in hotels, so she definitely did not want to fuck on top of that unless he was on the bottom, but still, she had a feeling they would both fight to be on top, given they were control freaks, and she knew they didn't have time for that.

She watched him in the mirror as he came up closer behind her, hesitating, not touching her at first, but she could feel his breath on her neck. And then his hands were on her, all over her, his hard cock pressed against her back. The sex took place with Heather's back to Dawn's husband, her hands on the desk, his hand on her hip, his other hand fumbling with the buttons on her silk blouse, pushing her bra up and over one breast so he could cup it as he fucked her from behind, his pants around his ankles (she assumed that was where they were, but she didn't look, and honestly didn't want to see if they were), her skirt pushed up and her underwear hanging off one ankle. It was messy and haphazard, which was the polar opposite of their shared work life . . . and exactly what Heather wanted and needed at that moment.

It was over as quickly as it had started. Efficiency was key for both of them. Heather came in a way that she hadn't before (or at least, couldn't remember doing). The intensity of her orgasm reminded her of the first time she swam in the ocean when she was a girl and got rolled under a wave; she couldn't catch her breath, but she didn't panic because it was quiet and it felt good in a way, and she knew that once it passed, she would breathe again, better than before, and she would be stronger because she'd survived. She'd overcome. And she would feel relief.

It had been so long since she felt relief.

He pulled out and they both caught their breath. He stumbled backward, sitting his bare ass on the bed, his pants still at his ankles, his half-limp cock still oozing cum on the bedspread.

Heather saw his reflection in the mirror over the desk on which she still leaned, and all she could think was *This is exactly why I do not touch bedspreads in hotels.*

She remained turned away from him as she reached down, pulled up her underwear, fixed her skirt, adjusted her bra, and buttoned her shirt. She turned to him then. He had pulled his pants up. They didn't make eye contact.

"I should go," he said.

"I'll get you those briefs—"

"No, um . . . no rush on that."

They gave each other a look. They both knew there was a rush and that Heather would have it to him first thing the next morning, if not that night. It annoyed her that he was suddenly treating her differently. Men were so fucking weak when it came to sex.

"See you at dinner," Heather said.

She didn't look at him as he grabbed his jacket and left.

They continued working together after that. They never spoke of the transgression, and neither of them made any further advances after that night. Frankly, Heather didn't really think about it again.

Until, that is, about four weeks later, when Heather realized her period was late. And she hadn't had sex with her husband since before their baby died six months earlier.

Fuck.

She slept with her husband that night and shared her pregnancy news with him three weeks after that. He would never know that this baby was not his, and Dawn's husband obviously could never know the baby was biologically his. He was just egomaniacal enough to want to claim it in some way, regardless of whose lives that blew up.

Maybe he was narcissistic enough to not put it together, but when he and Dawn also had their first baby around the same time, and then they all ended up going to the same private school, the Palms, years later and everyone remarked on how similar the boys looked, Heather knew she needed to protect her own family by getting them as far away as possible.

She hadn't been able to protect her first son, but she would protect her second: no one could know who his real father was.

So the only way to be sure of that, as far as Heather was concerned, was for her to get Dawn's husband fired. And disgraced. Which, frankly, was pretty easy to do because Dawn's husband had a million other strikes in his HR file. Heather was, for the most part, his only professional ally. And she took him down with one seemingly harmless call to HR.

Heather was nothing if not efficient and transactional.

Did she feel bad about the repercussions of her actions on Dawn and their family? For a moment. Sure. But Heather had to put her family first. And when she voiced her complaint to HR, Dawn's husband responded as she knew he would—an overreaction fueled with vehemence and zero self-control. And it was his response, not the small HR infraction she reported, that got him fired. She reminded herself of this fact when she caught Dawn glaring at her at school events . . . which was a lot.

So Dawn and her family left, fucked off to Canada, where Dawn was from, and now they were back. Here. In Los Angeles. In the same school. The boys, unknowingly half brothers, were friends and loved each other. But when people joked about their resemblance, it made Heather nervous. Heather was not someone who was accustomed to feeling nervous, and she didn't like it. At all.

Heather had given Dawn and her husband an out. A chance to start over. But they were back, and Heather couldn't have that.

So here she was at this woo-woo sound bath, which was supposed to be about "healing." Heather hated that word. *Healing.* How can something ever be truly healed if it leaves a scar, physical or emotional? "Healing" was a myth, if you asked her.

"Moving on" was more her style.

That said, it annoyed her sometimes when her son behaved in a way that was nonsensical to her (temper tantrums and such). She silently blamed Dawn's husband's genes. Heather's husband was remarkably even-tempered. He was also not their son's biological father. And no one could ever know that.

Dawn

Dawn sat in Milly's living room, surrounded by women, mothers like her, immersed in "healing energy." This should be her happy place, her "jam," but as she looked from Heather to Milly, all she felt was rage. So much rage.

Every time she thought she had breached the world of normalcy, Heather was there to push her back down into the cancellation underworld. Even though it was Milly who'd shared the news, Dawn was sure it was Heather keeping her out of the tennis club. It had to be. Who else would it be?

What had Dawn ever done to Heather?

If Heather weren't around, her husband would never have been canceled. If Heather weren't around, they would be happily ensconced in the tennis club. And yes, she'd pushed Milly for an answer, but she wished she hadn't told her about the tennis club. At least, not before the sound bath. She had been looking forward to this and now obviously couldn't enjoy it.

Dawn was not a violent person, but what she wanted, what she really wanted as the women moaned around her, was to kill Heather. And by *kill*, she didn't mean murder. She meant more like blow up her life. Kill her life. She wasn't sure yet how she was going to do it, but she would. She thought of that ugly needlepoint pillow her mother-in-law had at their house in Encino that said *Living well is the best revenge.* Dawn often wondered: Was living well really the best revenge? Or was, like, *revenge* the best revenge? She wanted Heather to suffer. To suffer like she and her family had.

But here she was at a sound bath, an event that would only capitalize on her two weaknesses, which were as follows:

> Silence. She hated it. Why did God invent talking if not to talk? It was like "reply all." She had to do it.
> Keeping her eyes closed. It made her feel like she was dying.

But she thought about what she'd learned when she was getting her life coach license, how one should accept and honor one's own weaknesses and see them as strengths. So on this particular night, during the sound bath, Dawn kept her head down so no one could see that her eyes were not closed as instructed.

It's interesting what you see when everyone else's eyes are closed!

Like sweet, perfect Milly, who was sidled up next to Eva. Almost too close. Or was Dawn reading into that?

Milly opened an eye, and Dawn quickly closed hers for a moment so as not to get caught watching. When she reopened them, she saw, with no uncertainty, Milly reaching for Eva's hand under a beige throw pillow . . . and Eva pushing her hand off and scowling at her. When Dawn gasped at the sight, Milly opened her eyes and caught Dawn watching her.

On one hand, Dawn was shocked! She wondered if it was sex, or love, or both. How long had it been going on? On the other hand, who fucking cared? What a scandal! She didn't need to be Milly's best friend and grovel and beg for help gaining admittance to the tennis club; she just needed Milly to know she knew what Milly clearly didn't want *anyone* to know.

Dawn smiled. She had made her weakness into her strength. She would win after all. Because something was going on with Eva and Milly, and she was the only one who knew.

And, fine, that may not be "leaning in" (sorry, Sheryl Sandberg), but this was something Dawn imagined Sheryl Sandberg also knew a little bit about . . .

Leverage.

Milly

Okay, seriously, how long was this sound bath going to last? As the singing bowls reached their (hopefully?) final crescendo, Seraphina encouraged everyone to howl with her. Even Milly's labradoodle howled from the other room, which made everyone laugh and open their eyes. Some women were teary, others joyful, all making eye contact with one another with a smile and a nod, as if they had been through something extraordinary together and were now bonded for life.

While Milly was happy that the sound-bath party-book party was a success, she worried about Dawn and what she'd actually seen (or, hopefully, hadn't seen—or at least, if she had seen, didn't think much of?). Milly's and Eva's hands had been under a throw pillow anyway. She thought of what her father, a titan of industry back in the day before he lost it all in an unfortunate stock buyout, had always told her to do when in doubt: "Deny, deny, deny!" He was wise, if, ultimately, a terrible businessman.

But still, she worried. Milly knew that Dawn was a climber on a good day, and this was not a good day. This was a bad, bad day. This was a day when Dawn was determined to get her family into the tennis club. Dawn (or her husband—or both) had created a formidable enemy in Heather for some reason, and Milly wanted to find out what that reason was. Milly felt empathy for Dawn, and her predicament, but also felt Dawn should have just stayed in Canada. Cut her losses! Why make it Milly's problem? Milly had enough problems. Why should she have to deal with Dawn's problems too?

"Were you still planning to stay to work on the Field of Dreams fundraising?" Milly asked Eva hopefully as they filed out of the living room and into the open-plan kitchen and dining room area.

"Unfortunately, I can't," Eva said. "Rain check?"

"Of course," said Milly. "Let me grab your coats."

"I'll help you." Eva followed her to the coatrack in the hallway. "What were you thinking?" she hissed.

"I'm so sorry. I wasn't . . . thinking. I was disappointed because we planned for you to stay after, and Mags wasn't supposed to be here—"

"Was I supposed to tell my wife she couldn't come with me?"

"That's not what I'm saying—"

"Milly, we need to cool off. Please don't text or call me unless it's school related."

"What? For how long?"

"For a while. Maybe forever. I don't know. This was not okay."

"You ready?" asked Mags sourly, appearing in the hallway. "Thanks, Milly. It was . . . interesting."

"Sure. Great to see you both," said Milly, holding back tears.

How would she ever shake off the rejection she felt from Eva? Or the anger and shame she felt at herself for making such a dumb mistake? How could she have tried to take Eva's hand at an event when her wife was sitting on her other side? So stupid, Milly! She knew better than that!

Was it over between them? She hated this feeling—the uncertainty, the potential heartbreak.

As Milly said goodbye to her guests and the last woman left, she started cleaning up, and tried to remind herself, through no shortage of tears, that tomorrow was a new day.

"Are you all right, Ms. Milly?" asked Guadalupe, emerging from the laundry room with a hamper of clean, perfectly folded clothes.

"Yes, thank you. I'm fine," said Milly, wiping her face and smiling. "Just a long night."

"I can wash those glasses for you."

"No, that's okay, Guadalupe. Thank you for everything. I'd be lost without you. You're the only one I can trust."

Guadalupe moved closer and held her, hugging her, rocking her gently as Milly cried.

"*Tranquila*, Ms. Milly," she whispered.

Milly whimpered and held tight to Guadalupe. Thank God for Guadalupe. She made a mental note to double the bonus she'd given her last year.

Once Guadalupe left, Milly set out to scrub her kitchen from top to bottom. She was a neat freak; cleaning her kitchen was her meditation, and she wouldn't sleep if she didn't leave it spotless before going to bed.

She scrubbed and scrubbed and thought through the night in a loop—about all the things she'd done wrong and what she should have done instead. She obviously should *not* have told Dawn about the club. That was a mistake. Also, taking Eva's hand in public? What was she thinking? She wanted to tell Eva about what Dawn had seen, but she was afraid to reach out to her, and definitely afraid Eva would end their relationship completely if she did. Milly had to fix this. Somehow.

Once the kitchen was clean and Milly's Ambien had started to kick in, she had the most amazing epiphany about her life and how to fix the Dawn/Eva situation, and suddenly everything was clear for her!

Yes! Tomorrow she would lsknv; ofqau hfq;oaifhaq bfhq;ioughqpogu rhqeopriu j h dgfsflz ioudfhiuibbakbfv;jbf;o euhg;ouah gv;aojdgh;qe ohg;aoighj

Ddddddygfl   uyfgliuy;pioy'[iuh'poujpoj/lih/olyhoiyh zjdhewwojhfBWJKALVN/WDEKJEFRTI3

TO: EVA MILLER
FROM: EVA MILLER
BCC: PALMS PARENTS, PALMS FACULTY
Subject: Update on New School Field and Noise Concerns

Dear Palms Community,

I am writing to provide you with an update regarding our new school Field of Dreams project. First, I would like to express our gratitude for your patience and understanding and ongoing financial support as we work to enhance our school facilities for the benefit of our students and the community. We are excited about the opportunities this new field will provide for our students to engage in outdoor activities and sports.

However, it has come to our attention that the new field has resulted in some inconveniences for our neighbors, particularly regarding noise disturbances. We are aware of the concerns raised by the residents of the adjacent building, and we are taking steps to address these issues.

Some of these steps may include more construction, including building a sound barrier, which would require more donations from our generous Palms community.

As we strive to create a positive and inclusive environment for all members of our community, we kindly ask for your continued cooperation, patience, and generosity, both of spirit and of funds.

Thank you for your continued support and understanding as we work towards making our Field of Dreams into a reality.

Warm regards,
Eva Miller
Principal, Palms School

TO: DAWN
FROM: DAWN

BCC: PALMS MOMMUNITY

Subject: Join Us for a Night of Mah-Jongg Fun Benefiting Our Field of Dreams Sound Barrier!

Dear Palms Mommunity,

I hope this email finds you well! As a proud member of our school mommunity, I'm excited to invite you to a special evening when we will put the "fun" in "fundraising" to raise money to construct a sound barrier so that our kids can play on our new Field of Dreams without disturbing our (very vocal!) neighbors.

A Night of Mah-Jongg is the perfect opportunity to come together, enjoy some friendly competition, and support a cause that's close to our hearts: the Palms School.

Whether you're a seasoned mah-jongg player or a complete novice, everyone is welcome to join in the fun! We'll have tables set up for players of all skill levels, so don't worry if you're new to the game.

In addition to the games, we'll also have refreshments and snacks to keep us energized and engaged throughout the evening.

Please RSVP to secure your spot, as space is limited. If you have any questions or need further information, feel free to reach out to me.

We can't wait to see you there!

Ciao,
Dawn

PART III

MAH-JONGG "MOM-JONGG" PARTY-BOOK PARTY
BENEFITING THE SOUND BARRIER FOR THE FIELD
OF DREAMS

Dawn

Dawn loved sharing the ancient game of mah-jongg with fellow moms. It was a game she had learned from her grandmother during the summers they would spend at her grandparents' lake house. It was the type of house where you could sit anywhere in a wet bathing suit and no one would yell at you. To this day, the smell of menthol cigarettes was comforting to her because her grandmother would have her three best friends over to play mah-jongg, and they'd chain-smoke (someone had always just quit or just started again). The women would arrive with a bottle of wine, some kind of casserole or dip, and their makeup and hair done. Dawn would watch as they reapplied their lipstick multiple times throughout the evening.

Dawn used to sit on the sectional couch in the living room, watching the women play at the wooden card table. Her grandmother kept whole walnuts in a large bowl with a big nutcracker on the coffee table, and while Dawn was allergic to nuts, she loved cracking them. It was satisfying and fun, and dangerous (even if it was just a mild allergy), and made her feel powerful. She would crack the shells and bring the nut-guts to the women playing mah-jongg, who would tell her how helpful and pretty she was. She loved everything about those evenings.

The women would laugh and gossip and complain about their husbands while the TV played *Dynasty* or *Dallas* in the background. Dawn was way too young to be watching those shows, and her mother never would have let her, but her grandmother had a much more laissez-faire attitude about childcare. What Dawn loved most about those evenings was seeing these women enjoying each other's company so much. The camaraderie—what Dawn now liked to call "mamaraderie." Laughing, playing, gossiping, commiserating, venting, supporting each other. Dawn dreamed of a time when she would cultivate her own group of friends and mamaraderie like the one her grandmother had in her mah-jongg group.

Dawn had joined a sorority in college for the express purpose of forging these types of female-friendship bonds, and yet she barely kept in touch with any of these friends outside of commenting on their social media posts from time to time. It was not for lack of trying on her part. That was why it was particularly hurtful to see posts of their annual reunions, to which she was not invited. It was like having a virtual front-row seat to a party she would never get to join.

But Dawn was not a dweller—she was a doer! She assumed she would find her female pack when she became a mom. As soon as she learned she was pregnant, she got on the wait list for *the* Mommy and Me group in Los Angeles, with an eye toward cultivating her own mommunity. After their weekly class—during which at least one baby shrieked the entire time and at least two women cried and at least one new mom blatantly lied, saying her newborn baby slept through the night and easily breastfed while the other women glared at her—they would all push their Bugaboo strollers to a café nearby and try to have conversations while also handling cranky newborns.

Dawn had heard of women who met lifelong friends in these baby groups. She hoped she would meet her lifelong friends in hers. She really tried! But it didn't happen for her. So, again, it was not for lack of trying on her part.

When their son started at the Palms, she loved the school, and she just knew that this was where she would find her mommunity, her pack, her coven, her gaggle of moms, who would get together every weekend to play mah-jongg in the backyard and drink rosé and talk about how great their kids and husbands and lives were.

Dawn tried. And tried. And tried. She really did. Some might even say she tried too hard, although she didn't think that was possible. But the friendships she expected, the friendships she wanted, the friendships she dreamed of . . . they just didn't take.

In true Dawn fashion, she did not give up. She showed up at every party-book party and every school event and field trip. But when her husband was forced to step down from his law firm, her world came crashing down. And it wasn't until they were living in Canada with her family that she learned it was Heather who had reported him to HR. She had tried so hard to be friends with Heather. Their boys loved each other—all the teachers said so. She'd reached out many, many times to organize a playdate for them, and Heather always had an excuse, always brushed her off, or sometimes wouldn't respond at all. It was infuriating. And confusing. And hurtful.

But here she was, back at the Palms, and throwing her own mah-jongg party-book party. It hadn't sold out like Milly's sound-bath party-book party, but a lot of moms had bought tickets. She thought of her grandmother and her grandmother's friends, and it made her smile. Her grandmother would be so proud of her. She thought about what she'd frequently told her one life coach client in Canada: "It's never too late to change your life." And just as it was never too late to change your life, it was never too late to make female friendships that would last a lifetime.

Dawn's grandmother used to say that mah-jongg was her favorite game because it required two things:

1.   Luck

But also . . .

2.   Skill

What was most remarkable about it for Dawn was how the strategies and rules for what had been originally created as a male-dominated gambling game centuries ago in China could so perfectly mirror those of modern-day private school momming in Los Angeles.

These were **Dawn's Mah-Jongg Rules**:

1. Have a clear plan of attack and stick with it.
2. But also be flexible!
3. If your strategy isn't working, be honest with yourself, and don't be afraid to pivot and change tactics.
4. Picking up tiles randomly is *not* strategy.
5. Be patient!
6. There are four players in every game, but you can control the decisions of only one of them: yourself.
7. *Trust no one.*

Number seven was the biggie. Especially now. Especially for Dawn. Especially in mah-jongg. And especially in life.

And especially since Heather had bought a ticket for her party that evening, and Dawn wondered if she would actually show up . . . And if so, why? Dawn was trying to focus on having a great party and raising money for the sound barrier for the Field of Dreams, but she couldn't help but wonder why Heather, who notoriously had wanted nothing to do with her, was coming to her mah-jongg party.

Milly

Milly was not excited about the mah-jongg (a.k.a. "mom-jongg") party-book party at the Palms that evening.

She did not know how to play mah-jongg. And while she definitely wasn't opposed to learning new things—she was actually *thrilled* to learn and to listen, of course, always listening—she just wasn't dying to learn about mah-jongg. Not tonight.

But Dawn was the host of the party and had asked her to come. Multiple times. And with Dawn having seen Milly attempting to hold Eva's hand the night of the sound bath, she knew it was best to stay on Dawn's good side.

Most importantly, all the money went to the school. To finishing the Field of Dreams! Or, now, to constructing a sound barrier so kids could actually play on the Field of Dreams. They had had to postpone the much-anticipated ribbon-cutting ceremony after neighbors in adjacent buildings had complained about the noise, posting crude signs on their balconies facing the school. It was a project Milly had been working on for years, and she was determined to see it through. It was for the kids, of course, but mostly Milly wanted to make Eva proud, to make Eva look great as the principal of this amazing school with an amazing new field. It would be her and Eva's legacy—their baby, if you will.

Since the sound-bath-party fiasco weeks before, Eva had not returned any of Milly's calls or texts (personal calls or texts, specifically;

Eva had replied, professionally and promptly, to any and all emails pertaining to the school and the annual giving fund and the Field of Dreams project).

Milly knew Eva would be at the mah-jongg party, and she was desperate to reconnect with her. She felt sure that if Eva saw her, she would soften and forgive her for doing something so risky as trying to hold her hand in public while her wife sat on her other side. Just thinking about it made Milly shudder. They had taken time off from seeing each other before, of course, but never because Eva was angry with Milly. They had to take breaks over the summer, when Eva would travel with her family. But they always found time to connect over text and over FaceTime. They told each other they loved each other. Milly had said it first, and immediately worried it might scare Eva. Eva didn't say it back right away, but once she did, Milly knew Eva meant it, and that filled her with joy and hope.

Milly was Eva's lieutenant, her "work wife," her confidante, her rock. She loved being the one Eva went to when she needed to vent about everything school related . . . and eventually, she vented to her about her marriage too. When she complained about Mags, Milly would try not to smile or be too hopeful, but to listen and nod sympathetically. She knew that was what Eva needed. And that was important: she did know what Eva needed, she gave her what she needed, and that was why she and Eva risked everything to be together. So why had she done something so stupid, so dangerous . . . so unnecessary at the sound-bath party?

Milly had to wonder—at least, she had to wonder once her therapist posed the question—where she saw her relationship with Eva going. Milly was never someone who imagined being one of those divorced parents. It just wasn't her style. And she and her husband were happy. Ish. Their marriage worked. They led separate lives, and he was a good dad when he needed to be, so she was okay with that. But now, after feeling all these feelings for Eva, and the devastation of not being able to communicate with her the last few weeks, she had to wonder if she wanted more from her. And whether that was possible.

Milly took an extra five minutes getting ready that night; she wore a vintage wrap dress and high wedges that made her legs look much longer than they were. Was it trying too hard for a moms-only mah-jongg tutorial in the school's multiuse auditorium? One hundred percent. But she was all about the female gaze these days, and she knew she had to get Eva's attention.

For Milly, the last few weeks had been miserable without Eva and their playful sexts and FaceTimes and, of course, their clandestine "meetings." Milly knew she had to change her attitude and get her head in the game. The Mah-Jongg Game, the Mom Game, the Eva Game. All the games.

As Milly walked into the Palms, she was unimpressed with the decor and the setup for the party-book party. Dawn had thrown ugly tablecloths on the Costco tables the school already had. Milly discreetly felt the tablecloth material between her thumb and index finger: coarse. Not surprising. She would have gotten a softer cloth. When would people learn? Texture matters.

Dawn ran over and greeted her. Milly smiled and hugged her. Dawn wasn't the only one who knew how to fake it.

"Can I get your opinion on something?" Dawn asked, pulling Milly into one of the nursery school classrooms closest to the entrance.

"Uh, sure," Milly said.

Dawn flipped on the fluorescent lights and closed the door to the classroom. Milly tried to act casual.

"Well, those are bright!" Dawn said. "The lights. Ugh."

Milly smiled. There was an awkward beat.

"The party looks great. The tablecloths are a nice touch," said Milly.

"Right? That means a lot, coming from you," Dawn said, putting her hand on her heart meaningfully.

"So, what's up?" asked Milly.

"Look, there's no easy way to say this, so I'll just . . . say it! I know something is going on with you and Eva."

"What?" Milly tucked her hair behind her ear and tried to smile like she had no idea what Dawn was talking about, like the notion was preposterous and shocking.

"I mean, it's obvious. And it's okay—"

"Of course there is something going on with Eva and me," she said, trying to sound confident but sounding defensive instead. "I have so many roles at this school. I consider her a dear friend—"

"Yes. And I think that one of those roles is more than friendly."

"Dawn! That's ridiculous!"

"Milly, I saw you. At the sound bath. You reached for her hand and she pulled it away. Pretty bold, what with her wife on the other side of her."

"I'm sorry, but I really don't know what you're talking about."

"I'm just saying . . . I would never say a word about what I saw . . ."

"There wasn't anything to see."

"This doesn't need to be painful. I am a vault! You can talk to me about this and I won't say anything to anyone. I promise!"

Milly stared at her.

"I want you to trust me. And confide in me. I'm your friend!" said Dawn.

Milly stepped back.

"What do you want, Dawn?"

"I want your trust! I want your friendship."

"That's all?"

"Yes! And . . . also . . . just . . . a small favor. Our membership to the tennis club approved."

Dawn put her palms together under her chin, her index fingers touching the middle of her smiling lips.

"Dawn, I can't reverse a decision that the membership committee made."

"Actually, a member—that would be you—can appeal."

"Me?"

"Yes. I need a member to get twenty other member signatures supporting the appeal. I'm sure you could do that for me . . . and my family. I did some researching after you told me the news at the sound bath. You have great internet access in your powder room, by the way."

Milly knew she was trapped.

"Of course. I'd be happy to."

"Where there's a will, there's a way! That's what I always tell my It's Always Darkest Before the Dawn life-coaching clients!"

"It's a . . . great saying," Milly offered.

"Right? Well, I am so glad we had this chat! Maybe we can do dinner soon? Just you and me? Or invite some other moms along? The more the merrier!"

Milly nodded and smiled.

"Okay, I'd better get back to the party. Oh, and you're in my mah-jongg group!"

"I'll be in in a minute," Milly said sweetly.

"I'm so glad we had a chance to talk about this. I was so nervous. Can you believe that? Because I didn't want to come across like threatening, you know? I promise you my lips are sealed. I will protect your secret with my life. You can tell me anything!"

Dawn clapped her hands, shrugged, and left the classroom.

Milly sat down on the edge of the classroom table. Fuck. Now she'd have to mobilize and get *twenty* signatures to put Dawn and her family back in front of the membership committee. She'd have to promise a *lot* of free meals at her husband's restaurants, but she guessed it was worth it to protect her marriage. And Eva's. Milly took a deep breath—*"Tranquila"*—as she walked out of the classroom and back into the multipurpose room, where the party was underway.

Jillian

Jillian arrived at the mah-jongg party-book party a few minutes late because she'd been busy FaceTime-fucking her daughter's teacher, Flynn Hartshorn, from her minivan. She'd parked a few blocks away from the school, where she could have some privacy; though, to be honest, it was the danger of someone seeing her in her minivan with her hands in her pants while Flynn watched over FaceTime that made it that much more exciting.

She preferred that to fucking in the un-air-conditioned one-bedroom apartment he shared with his college frat brother from ASU (which she had done only once and wasn't rushing back). She'd never even been to Arizona, let alone thought she would ever fuck someone who went to its state school. She was Ivy League material. She had turned down Stanford, for crying out loud!

Jillian thought if only Flynn were half as good at teaching as he was at fucking, there wouldn't be a petition going around to have him fired. Maybe it was for the best; she needed to end this thing soon. As much pleasure as it had given her over the last few weeks, it was wrong, and the whole sneaking-around thing was frankly exhausting.

She couldn't escape the feeling that this fling with Flynn had, intentionally or unintentionally, "woken her up"—sexually, emotionally—from her midlife malaise, and now she felt like she was a teenager again. When she looked in the mirror, she liked what she saw. Her cheeks were flushed, her eyes somehow sparkled. If one could "see" collagen, she felt it was coursing—nay, *oozing*—through her like it had when she was younger.

She used any opportunity to get out of the house or to get her husband and kids out of the house so she could FaceTime with Flynn and her vibrator. She knew she wasn't giving her kids the attention they needed or deserved, but this wouldn't be forever, she assured herself.

And the weirdest part? It seemed to be helping her marriage; at least, in her husband's eyes, it was. She was now so horny all the time—she thought about sex constantly, she wanted to orgasm constantly—that she had sex with her husband sometimes more than once in a day, which, for a married couple of almost twenty years, was a lot more than the once-every-month-or-two (they went as long as six months once!) sex they'd been having before that.

Jillian marveled at how easy it was for men to feel reconnected through sex. Sex did not make her feel reconnected; she just felt . . . satisfied . . . and then guilty . . . but also not . . . but also very.

She did enjoy sex more now with her husband. She didn't even need CBD lube. But that may have been because she was thinking about Flynn. Which also made her feel guilty and kind of like she was cheating on both of them.

As Jillian walked into the mah-jongg party-book party in the Palms School multipurpose area, relaxed and blushing, Flynn was still texting her about how hard she'd made him cum, and she thought she'd have to tell everyone she was on a new SSRI or a higher dose of her estrogen patch, which, shit, she realized in that moment she'd forgotten to change. What day of the week was it, again? Was her estrogen patch even still adhered to her body? She was supposed to change it every three days, but she couldn't even remember the last time she had done so.

She had named Flynn's contact card in her phone after a childhood best friend's maiden name and then muted it in case he texted her when she was with her husband or kids (which was a lot). When she had told her friend that she was using her name for her affair's contact card, her friend laughed and said that a few of her other friends were also using her name for the exact same purpose. That annoyed Jillian because it made her feel a little less special, like she was less of a maverick. She needed to feel special. But also, it made her feel better—vindicated, almost—that there were other perimenopausal women out there rediscovering their sexuality, having fun, taking risks, and behaving badly. She felt a little less alone and a little less guilty about what she was doing.

But the guilt was always there. The baseline was always guilt. Fear too. But she was feeling things again. And feeling things, like really feeling them, was intoxicating! And that was also dangerous and exciting. Her banal middle-aged anxiety had been replaced by real fear of blowing up her life and her family. Of course she didn't want her husband to find out. And of course she didn't want to be with Flynn long term, but she had become addicted to the adrenaline as if it were heroin.

So, why was she here? She had very little interest in learning to play mah-jongg, but Eva had not returned her last two emails and Jillian wanted some guidance after her daughter had done so poorly on the ISEEs. Her daughter was so proud of how hard she'd studied, and so proud of having taken them, and felt she had done so well. She hadn't. So would—or should—they submit the scores? Or was this all just a terrible, morale-crushing, expensive experiment?

Dawn had promised her that Eva was coming to this party-book party, so she paid the seventy-five dollars to attend and here she was . . . and no Eva in sight.

Fuck.

"Jillian!" yelled Dawn, rising from a four-person table in the middle of the room.

Jillian smiled, hoping to keep moving, but Dawn waved her over maniacally. Dawn was perfectly nice, but she tried so hard all the time. And it was exhausting.

"Jillian, you're with us! You're at our table!"

Dawn stood with Milly. Why was Milly in a dress and wedges? Had she gotten a blowout? For mom-jongg?! She could be so weird. Jillian was already regretting her decision to come to this. But she grinned through her gritted teeth and headed over, scanning the crowd in search of Eva.

Heather

Heather should have been at the club playing tennis.

But instead, here she was, walking into the Palms for a stupid mah-jongg party-book party. The reason for this was simple: she'd heard that Dawn was trying to appeal the club-membership decision Heather had forced, and she suspected Milly might know more or even be helping with the twenty signatures needed for the appeal. Heather was not afraid of confrontation, so she decided to go someplace she knew she could get answers.

Most importantly, things were getting worse at school, and so she could not risk Dawn's family infiltrating their club. Just the day before, the new teacher, Flynn Hartshorn or whatever, had called her to say that her son had vomited during their ukulele elective. Heather's husband had been unreachable (even if she had a bigger job and made more money than he did, she was always called first and expected to keep her phone on at all times, while he was not), so she ran out of her office, missing an important conference call and several billable hours she would have to make up at some point, just to get to the school to pick up their son.

But when she'd gotten to the Palms, she realized that the sick kid Flynn had called her about was *Dawn's son*, not hers. Flynn apologized for the mistake, but couldn't stop talking about how alike the two boys looked.

"Are you *sure* they're not related?" he'd asked multiple times.

Heather had wanted to kill him.

When Heather arrived at the Palms that night, she inserted herself at the table where Milly and Dawn were sitting.

"You're not at this table," Dawn said through gritted teeth and a forced smile.

"I am now," Heather said, and sat down.

Heather would be lying if she didn't admit that she enjoyed watching Dawn squirm.

"Milly," Heather said, "I've been trying to reach you."

Milly glanced up from her phone briefly and then looked back down. Heather noticed that she was uncharacteristically distracted.

"I know I owe you a call. I'm sorry. The whole Field of Dreams–sound barrier debacle has been a lot . . ." Milly trailed off and went back to her phone.

As they started picking and organizing their tiles, Heather noticed that both Milly and Jillian were checking their phones. Constantly. Sometimes smiling, sometimes frowning. In addition to being annoying, it was unsportsmanlike, a trait that was aggravating to Heather. Even though she didn't even know how to play the game yet, it appeared that these two women were cheating together.

Who would cheat at mah-jongg when there was no money at stake?

"The rule is, no phones," said Heather.

Neither Milly nor Jillian looked up. Heather and Dawn looked at each other. They both coughed suggestively and stared at them. Finally, Dawn and Heather agreed on something.

Milly and Jillian, both startled, looked up and apologized profusely.

"My son has a cold."

"My daughter is . . . dyslexic."

"A mother's work . . ." Heather said sarcastically.

They all forced smiles.

"So, shall we continue?"

Everyone nodded . . . and started playing again . . . but within seconds, Milly and Jillian were back on their phones.

"Okay, seriously, are you two, like, cheating with each other?"

Milly, almost in tears, stared at Jillian, who was suddenly sheet white.

"Cheating?"

"I don't even know how to play this game, so I wouldn't know where to start with cheating."

"Then let us see your texts," said Heather.

Both Milly and Jillian held their phones to their chests.

"I am not showing you my phone," Jillian said.

"I'm leaving," said Heather.

"But . . . we need four people to play," said Dawn.

"I have an early morning at work tomorrow."

Heather dumped her tiles back into the box as Dawn gasped. Without ceremony, Heather stood up and walked out. This was a waste of time. She had work to do. She had hoped to confront Milly, but it was clear she wasn't getting any answers tonight that she couldn't find herself at the club this weekend.

Milly

How was Milly supposed to sit through a game of mah-jongg while Eva was just a floor above, waiting for her? Just as she was picking her tiles, Eva had texted her cryptically to meet in her office after she was done. She'd said she had something important to discuss. Milly wanted to go to her, to touch her, to hug her, to apologize, to promise she'd be more careful, more secretive. She wanted Eva to kiss her, to absolve her, to tell her everything was going to be okay.

That was one of the crazy things about being a mom: you get so used to making everything okay for everyone else that if someone does it for you, even the littlest thing, it's like the most beautiful, most magical of tricks.

Once Heather had left, making it impossible to continue the game, Milly took the opportunity to excuse herself.

"I'm just going to run to the loo," she said.

Milly looked to where the security guard, Reggie, sat by the stairs leading to the second floor. Normally, Reggie would not allow anyone past the first floor in the evening, but he was used to Milly and Eva working late into the night, and thus Milly gave him a warm hug and moved right past him and upstairs.

Milly entered Eva's office as she had so many times before. She knew every inch and angle of it. Eva sat behind her desk, the glow of her desk lamp reminding Milly of all those Zoom town halls years ago, when her attraction to and obsession with Eva had begun. She had always admired Eva's focus, especially when it was concentrated on her, but now Eva was so focused on her laptop that she did not even acknowledge Milly.

Milly shifted her weight from one foot to the other, uncomfortable with this feeling of being ignored by Eva. She felt vulnerable. Invisible.

"How was the mah-jongg?" Eva asked without looking up.

Oh.

Oh, Milly thought.

Okay.

Were they pretending everything was normal?

Milly sat down in the chair in front of Eva's desk, making sure her skirt rode up as she did.

"It wasn't terribly well organized. My group was also not . . . cohesive. But it seemed like it made money for the sound barrier, so that's what's important. Of course."

There was a beat. Milly felt like a student must feel when they were called to the principal's office for doing something wrong. Milly bit her bottom lip. She crossed her legs and tried to seem casual.

Eva kept typing, then took a deep breath, closed her computer, sat back, took off her readers, and rubbed her eyes before looking up and making eye contact with Milly for the first time in what seemed like months.

Milly sucked in her breath and silently reminded herself: *Tranquila.*

"Hi," said Eva. She smiled.

Milly's heart soared. Maybe she wasn't mad anymore?

"Hi," said Milly.

They stared at each other.

"I'm sorry!" Milly blurted out.

Eva shook her head. She got up from her Herman Miller Aeron desk chair, and she moved around to the front of her desk and leaned against it. Milly leaned forward, crossing her arms to push her breasts up, ready for whatever Eva wanted to do to her, or for her to do to Eva. This was the moment Milly had been waiting for since the sound-bath fiasco. This was the longest they had gone without seeing each other or talking secretly since this phase of their relationship started.

"Milly, we both knew when this started that it wasn't forever."

Milly's heart fell. She knew where this was going. But it couldn't. She wouldn't let it. She realized in that moment that she couldn't—wouldn't—live without Eva.

"You taking my hand at the sound bath . . . with Mags on the other side of me—"

"I know, I know. It won't happen again. I texted you that. It was a dumb mistake. It was reckless. I'm sorry! Let me make it up to you—"

Milly stood up on her ridiculous wedges. On top of getting dumped, she was definitely going to break an ankle.

Eva held up her hand.

"No. Milly, this has to end. It was fun and crazy, and we both had our reasons for doing this even though we both knew it was wrong—*is* wrong—and how much damage this could do to people we love—innocent people."

"But—"

"I don't regret it, Milly. And maybe in a different world, in another place, we could be together, but—"

"No, Eva—"

"You and I both know this can't continue. What happened at the sound bath was a real wake-up call for me. I've done some serious thinking over the last few weeks, and this is how it has to be. I value our friendship and our working relationship too much to let this go on and hurt either of us—or worse, hurt our families."

Milly sat down, crushed. She crumpled over, her head in her hands. It was like Eva, in all her Eva-ness, had sparked something in Milly. For the first time, Milly was more than the mother-wife-PTA-class-mom-head-of-fundraising-committee. Eva gave her passion and hope and excitement. When she was with Eva, she felt like the hand of the queen. And now it was back to her sleepy little mom life. It was, of course, the life she had always wanted (not knowing it would be so sleepy or that she would want more, want something completely different), but now this perfect life just seemed not enough if she couldn't be with Eva.

She couldn't help but imagine a world in which they were together, a world in which they both left their spouses and blended their families. People did that! It wasn't like they would be pioneers!

Eva bent down, putting her hand on Milly's cheek. Milly leaned her head into Eva's hand and looked up at her desperately. This couldn't be over. She wouldn't let it. This was just a blip.

She knew what she had to do.

Jillian

Well, that was embarrassing. Jillian guessed it could have been even more embarrassing had anyone actually seen the dirty sexts she was receiving, detailing all the things he wanted to do to her as she was trying to learn fucking mah-jongg.

It had been a crazy few weeks. More than crazy. Exciting. Sexy. She felt alive, awake. She felt excited; she felt attractive and womanly. She felt like she wanted to be touched, that she was excited to be touched, which was not something she had felt in a long time. Even her husband had a spring in his step from all the sex they were having, and it was . . . endearing. Could it be possible that her affair was bringing her and her husband closer? Or was she conflating the immense guilt she felt about her affair with a renewed commitment to and love for her marriage?

Of course she knew she could not keep this up. She knew this could blow up her life. On one hand, she felt entitled to it. Like, she'd kept her part of the bargain in this marriage until then, but he had not. She should be allowed this transgression. But also, she knew that was an excuse. She knew it wasn't a fair comparison, and she was not a cheater by nature. At least, she'd never thought she was or could be— but actually, maybe she was.

Was this a midlife crisis?

It felt like she was in someone else's body. And whoever's body this was, it felt too good to stop.

But she had to stop. She knew that (logically). Plus, it seemed like Flynn was getting too attached and was probably going to get fired. She didn't want to seem like part of the firing squad, or who knew how he might react.

Jillian had been hoping to see Eva at the mah-jongg party, but she was probably hiding out. Could she be hiding in her office? Maybe she could catch her off the clock—if Eva ever actually *was* off the clock. It seemed she lived and breathed for the power she had as principal.

Jillian decided she would go upstairs to see if Eva was there. She wasn't sure what she'd say or do, what assurances she wanted or needed, or what Eva could even give her (aside from the usual bullshit) with regard to her daughter's admissions journey, but she had to try.

The stairs to the second floor were guarded by beloved security guard Reggie, who had been working at the Palms for decades.

"Reggie, do you mind if I run upstairs to use the faculty bathroom, please? This one's locked and I really need it."

"Sorry, ma'am, no one upstairs."

Jillian smiled warmly.

"Reggie, I don't want to get too graphic here, but I birthed two nine-pound babies. When I need to go, I can't hold it for long . . ."

Reggie was not amused and seemed uncomfortable, which made Jillian feel a little guilty, but whatever. He shook his head and turned a blind eye as she went up the stairs.

As she walked down the second-floor hallway, she noticed a light on in Eva's office and headed toward it.

She tiptoed up to the side of Eva's office door and looked in:

No one was there.

Huh.

She entered, thinking how easy it would be to send an email from her computer to the head of the school where her daughter wanted to go. She felt confident she could impersonate Eva's haughty principal tone.

She contemplated doing it, but understood the many ways it could backfire. Plus, it felt like someone was watching her. She shrugged it off because what she had said to Reggie about birthing two nine-pound babies was, for better or worse, true. Also, she maybe had a UTI from all the sex she'd been having. Basically, she really had to pee.

She made her way into the faculty bathroom, which had three stalls.

Instinctually, she avoided the handicapped stall because it was bad form and obviously bad karma to use it when someone was not actually disabled . . . or handi-abled? Differently abled? She didn't know what was or wasn't offensive anymore. She went into one of the narrow regular stalls. But then, she knew she was the only one upstairs, so fuck form and fuck karma . . . She was going to treat herself to the more spacious stall.

She put the toilet seat cover down and she sat. Staring at her phone as she peed, she scrolled through her Instagram feed. She heard the door to the bathroom open. Fuck. She hoped it wasn't Eva or she'd definitely be in trouble for using the handicapped stall when she wasn't handicapped . . . maybe even canceled! Would Eva tell the schools to which she was applying her daughter that her mother was the type of person who used the handicapped stall when not handicapped? Would it keep her daughter from getting into private school? Shit. Why hadn't she just used the regular stall? What was wrong with her?

She heard the footsteps pass and enter the stall next to her.

She would just wait it out. The stall was comfortably spacious, after all.

"Pssst."

Jillian looked around.

"Up here."

Jillian looked up to see Flynn watching her pee from above the partition between the stalls, his chin resting on his hands, his eyebrows raised.

"Of all the faculty bathrooms in all the world, you had to come into mine," he said with a smirk.

"Flynn! What are you doing in here?" she whispered as she struggled to wipe and pull her pants up.

"I just wanted to catch you with your pants down."

"Gross."

Sometimes—actually, all the time these days—she really wondered what she was doing. "What are you even doing here?"

"My roommate is thruppling again. So . . . not a lot of room for Flynn."

"Did you just refer to yourself in third person—"

"Besides, there's a beanbag chair in my classroom I have my eye on. It has to be more comfortable than my futon."

"Flynn, you can't sleep in your classroom!"

"Why not?"

"Because this is a school . . . not a hotel. You're a teacher. I should not have to explain this to you!"

"How about *I* explain some things to *you?*" he said, trying to flirt, though the line didn't really land or make any sense.

"You should go home. Why don't you, like, quaddle with them?"

"What's a quaddle?"

"I assumed four people having sex was a *quaddle* if three is a *thrupple.*"

"I don't think so. I haven't heard that terminology before. I've had orgies, obviously—like, who hasn't . . . but . . . I don't do them when I have a girlfriend."

He put one leg over the stall and then the other, then tumbled down as she was buttoning her jeans. He landed in front of her with a goofy smile.

"I didn't know you had a girlfriend. You should stay at her house, then—"

"Duh. I'm talking about you."

Well, this was not good. In fact, it all just got very, very bad.

"I'm not your girlfriend, Flynn. I'm married. Happily. Or . . . whatever."

"Yeah, but, like, I can make you *actually* happy. I know how. I like to make you happy—"

"There's a difference between making a woman orgasm in a car or on a futon or on FaceTime and being her partner in life—"

He put his finger to her lips.

"Flynn—"

"SHHHHH," he said.

Jillian wondered how she'd gotten here. All the missteps. There'd been so many that it was just a blinding blur of fuckups.

It was bad enough that she had used the handicapped stall when she wasn't actually handicapped or differently abled or whatever she was supposed to call it . . . but now she was in there, at school, with her daughter's teacher, with whom she was having an affair?

He moved closer to her so that her back was against the wall of the stall with the handicap bar on it. He put one arm on the wall next to her, leaning in (*not that kind of leaning in*), and put his other hand on her face, tucking her hair behind her ear.

And that was when he started humming softly in her ear.

"Are you humming Ed Sheeran?"

"He's the voice of my generation."

She raised an eyebrow.

"You're not really in a position to critique my music choices, Spice Girl."

He had a point.

And before she could cry or laugh or protest, he put both his hands under her, effortlessly lifting her up so that her legs were open around his waist and her ass rested on the handicapped bar.

This was all so wrong. But she didn't stop it. She couldn't. She didn't want to. All the lines were blurred in that moment. Could. Should. Would.

Wood!

He was so fucking hard.

She couldn't help but gasp. Fucking Flynn. Fucking Ed Sheeran.

He kissed her deep and slow. She knew his tongue now. She thought about it when it wasn't in her mouth, or on her body, or inside her. He pulled back and looked at her.

"Your husband doesn't fuck you like I do."

"In a handicap stall? He would never."

"Accessible," he lisped with his tongue deep in her ear.

"What?" she asked, out of breath.

"You can't say 'handicap.' It's not inclusive language. You say 'accessible,'" he said as he pulled her pants off and went down on her until she almost came . . . She was right there, on the brink . . . How did he know? He was really not that smart . . . but somehow he knew . . . exactly how to make her feel good. And when he came up to kiss her, she was in a fog of bliss and desire; however . . . she couldn't help but notice . . .

Her small, clear, rectangular estrogen patch was now stuck in Flynn's man bun. It was time for a new one anyway.

He fucked her until they came together. And they stayed like that for a beat, breathing heavy, with him inside her, her bare ass on the cold stainless steel *accessible* railing thing—a constant reminder that she was a terrible, horrible person in every possible way and would probably, definitely be canceled (also in every possible way) and be going straight to hell and have terrible karma . . . But fuck if she didn't feel good, if she didn't feel euphoric, in that moment.

Once it was over, she deftly pulled her estrogen patch out of his man bun and threw it in the toilet without him even noticing.

She made a note to herself to put on a new one after she showered when she got home that night.

"I love you, Jillian," Flynn whispered in her ear.

Uh-oh.

For not the first time that night, she realized this, whatever *this* was, had gone too far. Jillian pulled away and looked him in the eye sternly.

"Flynn, you don't love me. You just love fucking me."

"No, I love you. I really love you. I've never felt this way about anyone before. When I told my mom about you, she—"

"You told your *mom*? Did you tell her my *name*—"

Jillian extricated herself from the wall he had her pinned against, and the handicapped banister that was definitely not meant for fucking one's daughter's teacher on, and she got dressed as quickly as she could.

"I tell her everything. She's the best. You'd love her—"

"Flynn, you're a really nice guy—"

"You remind me of my mom. Like, not in a weird way—"

"There is *only* a weird way! Look, let's just go back to you being my daughter's teacher."

"I can't go backward."

"Flynn, it's not backward; it's forward. You are . . . great—"

"You said that already—"

"And I'm sure one day you'll be a great teacher—"

"What do you mean, 'one day'?"

"And you'll meet someone your own age—"

"Age is just a number—you said so on your Instagram."

"You've been looking through my Instagram?"

"No."

She stared at him.

"Whatever, I looked at your Instagram. What's the big deal?"

"That's kind of stalking."

"It's not stalking if it's my girlfriend."

"But I'm not that. Definitely . . . not that."

"Are you breaking up with me?"

"Can't break up with you if we're not together, Flynn. I don't know how to be any clearer on this—"

"I know why you're freaking out. Love is scary—"

Jillian tried to button her jeans and extricate herself from Flynn and from the stall and the situation all at once.

"Flynn, right now, honestly, *you* are scary. I have a family. I need to get my daughter into middle school, and earn a living, and make dinner . . . Fuck, I forgot to take the mac and cheese out of the freezer!"

Distracted and annoyed with herself, she started texting her husband directions for defrosting the mac and cheese.

"I love mac and cheese," said Flynn, tucking Jillian's hair behind her ear. She pushed him away.

"This has to be over. Now. Okay?"

"Do you think if we were a celebrity couple, they would call us *Flynnian*?"

Jillian was on the verge of a complete anxiety attack. Trying to have this postcoital conversation with Flynn was like talking to someone who spoke a different language, or trying to reason with a toddler. Or trying to reason with a toddler who spoke a different language.

She just wanted to get the fuck out of this stall and this bathroom and this school, and push the reset button on the last few weeks of her life.

"Where is all this negativity coming from all of a sudden?" he asked.

"It's coming from . . . *everywhere*! You knew I was married. You are my kid's fucking teacher, for fuck's sake. Please. Don't call me. Don't text me. Let's just . . . be professional from now on."

"Don't leave. I don't want us to go to sleep angry."

Her eyes widened. This was, for lack of better Ivy League words, *not good*.

"I just want to be really clear. I'm not angry," she said as calmly as she could muster.

"Okay, phew."

"But it *is* over between us, okay?"

"We'll just talk tomorrow. When you've cooled off."

She had to get out of there.

She said, "Okay. Okay, so, bye."

Jillian unlocked the stall and went to push the door out, but instead it pulled in, and so she had to back into Flynn, who thought this was

Jillian trying to start something sexual again, which was definitely *not* what she was going for, but she got the door opened finally and extricated herself from what felt like his octopus arms (they were everywhere!), and out she went.

She had to get Flynn out of that school.

Maybe he could just . . . disappear? Or die?

Okay, obviously, not really *die*, but disappear?

Or . . . as Jillian went down the stairs, she had an idea.

At the bottom of the staircase, she stopped by Reggie's desk.

"Hey, Reggie, I think I saw someone upstairs in one of the classrooms," she said. "Maybe you should check it out?"

Reggie's eyebrows shot up in surprise. "Thanks for letting me know. I'll take care of it right away."

Jillian felt bad setting Flynn up to be fired, but she also felt she didn't have a choice. Sure, she had gone into this relationship willingly, but it had gone too far. He'd told his mom about her?! She told herself he'd forget about her. He'd move on. She just had to cut ties. No big deal. Everything would be fine. She opened his contact card and blocked him as she walked out of the school.

Milly

Milly and Eva had moved down the hallway from Eva's office and into the kitchen to get tissues and a glass of water for Milly, who couldn't stop crying.

Milly wouldn't let this happen. It couldn't be over. She wouldn't let it. She went from feeling numb to desperate to angry and back to desperate.

"You've meant so much to me, Milly. And the good news is that our friendship doesn't have to change. Your work for the school doesn't have to change. Everything else can stay the same."

"Except us. Except . . . you and me."

"Correct."

"Can't we just be us . . . a little longer?"

"We're like Icarus—"

"We fucked too close to the sun?"

"Basically, yeah. We just can't risk hurting our families."

"I know you're right, but I'm not ready for it to be over."

"Get a hold of yourself, Milly. We were always friends. It was always a friendship with us underneath it all. The other stuff was icing on the cake."

Milly nodded in agreement. She loved icing. And, fine, she would give it up forever, but she needed one more night with Eva. She kept nodding, her chin quivering, her mouth turning upside down into what she assumed was a very, very ugly cry, but she couldn't help it. She had never felt so strongly about anything or anyone before.

"Honey . . ." Eva moved to hug Milly.

Milly pushed her away. "Don't! I'm fine."

"This is hard for me too."

"Really? Because it seems pretty fucking easy for you."

"Milly? Look at me."

Milly stared down at the floor. She felt like a reject. She felt like a fool. She wished she could go back in time and live in that first COVID kiss with Eva in their unpermitted guesthouse forever.

"Milly. I love you."

Milly watched a tear drop from Eva's eye, landing on Milly's bare leg. She wiped it away with her hand and wiped her eyes. She looked up at Eva.

"Then why are you doing this?"

"I'm doing it for us. It's like we've both been driving blind . . . and at some point, one of us has to watch the road or we're going to crash and innocent people are going to get hurt."

Milly knew Eva was right. She was always right. But it hurt so much. It hurt in a way she had never hurt before. It hurt in a way she didn't know if she would ever recover or be able to move on from. Of course Milly had had her heart broken when she was younger. But this was something else. It was the realization that this beautiful connection, this feeling, had to stop.

And she now knew how rare, how *never again*, that feeling was.

Milly let Eva hug her. They continued to hug until their cheeks touched, and Milly felt that heat, that heat only Eva made her feel. Was this the last time she'd feel it?

She wrapped her arms around Eva's waist, then moved her hands up her sides, and to her neck and her face until their lips met.

"Milly, we can't," Eva said.

But for the first time in their relationship, Milly was the one in charge. She needed to be with Eva, to show her how much she had learned from her. When she'd first gone down on Eva, she was so nervous, so embarrassed; she had no idea what to do. But Eva had taught her. Eva wasn't embarrassed or shy; she knew what she liked and wanted, and she asked for it. But now it was Milly's turn. She wanted to show her the student had become the teacher; she wanted Eva to know what she would be missing.

They kissed and kissed and held each other, and Milly made Eva come multiple times. And while Eva reiterated that they could not continue after this, that this was the last time, they were both wholly there in those moments. And it was beyond thrilling for Milly.

"We should get back," said Eva. Milly nodded.

As they walked out of the kitchen and back toward Eva's office, however, they caught movement in the hall. Someone was upstairs? They hid behind a wall and peeked around the corner to see:

Reggie.

What was he doing upstairs, and had he seen anything? Eva leaned back against the wall, and Milly could tell she was starting to panic.

"This is exactly why I wanted to stop, Milly!" she whispered.

"I'm sure he didn't see anything," said Milly, surprised at her own confidence and calm.

"Who's there? I should tell you I'm armed and I don't have my glasses on."

"Reggie, it's us. Eva and Milly. Everything okay?"

Eva came around the corner with her arms raised.

"I was told there was someone in one of the classrooms, so I came to check it out."

"Thanks, Reggie. Just us, I think," said Eva.

At which point, they all heard a sound—was it a ukulele? It was coming from a classroom down the hall.

Reggie put his finger to his lips and held up his gun.

"Is the gun really necessary?" asked Eva.

"I was LAPD for years. Trust me."

They tiptoed over to one of the sixth-grade classrooms and peeked in, only to see Flynn, cuddled up in one of the oversize beanbags with his sweatshirt over him, strumming his ukulele.

Reggie put his gun away. "What the . . . ?"

Eva stormed into the classroom with Milly and Reggie at her heels. She flipped on the lights and Flynn sat up, remarkably nonplussed by being discovered.

"Flynn, just what do you think you're doing in the classroom after school hours?"

"Oh, well, I was uh . . . working late. And so I figured I'd just sleep here. I have an early morning, anyway. I'm dedicated to the job!"

"You can't sleep at school!" Milly blurted out.

"Milly, please. I'll handle this," Eva said, looking around the classroom. "Okay, Flynn, I've tried very hard to make this work with you. I have tremendous pressure from parents to let you go—"

"Which parents?"

"—but sleeping in your own classroom is . . . well, it speaks to a lack of judgment . . . and basic common sense . . . that I just can't condone."

"What are you saying?"

"I'm saying please pack your things and go. I don't think the Palms is the right school for you."

"Wait. Are you . . . firing me?"

"Yes, I am."

"Like, really?"

"Yes, really."

"You're firing me for my dedication to the job?"

"I'm firing you because it is a violation for anyone to sleep in the school, and a teacher should know that that is not appropriate behavior."

Flynn shrugged. "Does it actually say in the rules somewhere that I can't sleep at school?"

"It's a given!" said Milly.

"Let's go. Up. Reggie can walk you out. No one wants drama or humiliation."

Flynn shrugged and sighed. He got up out of his beanbag chair and walked toward Reggie, high-fiving him. "My man."

"Sorry, Flynn," said Reggie.

"We all answer to someone, you know what I mean? Truth to power." Flynn raised his arm with his hand in a fist and walked out of the classroom, followed by Reggie, as Eva and Milly stood in the classroom in shock.

Milly could not believe what had just happened. All of it. And now she'd get to help Eva draft her email about Flynn's termination. Flynn's bad behavior had brought them together . . . for the time being, at least.

Dear Palms Parents,

It is with mixed emotions that I announce the departure of Flynn Hartshorn from our school faculty. In his brief tenure at the Palms, he has been an integral part of our educational team, and his dedication to and passion for teaching have made a significant impact on our sixth-grade students' lives. While we are sad to see him go, we understand and support his decision and wish him the very best.

In the interim, I am pleased to announce that Lucille Jackson, our PE teacher of twenty years, will be stepping in as the temporary sixth-grade teacher. Lucille is a seasoned educator with decades of experience and a deep commitment to our school community. She will ensure continuity in your child's education and provide a supportive learning environment during this transition period.

Thank you for your continued support and partnership in your child's education.

Warm regards,
Eva Miller
Principal, Palms School

TO: MILLY
FROM: MILLY
BCC: PALMS COMMUNITY
Subject: Join us for our annual Glamping Adventure!
Dearest Palms Families,

It's that time of year again: another memorable glamping trip to El Capitan Canyon! Many of you have joined in past years and you know how much fun it is! And for those of you who have never come before, and are maybe a little nervous about "glamping," don't be! The cabins have heat and are actually very nice. I mean, they're no George V in Paris, but they're super cozy (and did I mention there will be wine?!)!

Who doesn't need to disconnect from the hustle and bustle of everyday life and reconnect with nature and each other? I also want to mention it is the weekend after our sixth-grade class hears from middle school admissions, so we will have a lot to celebrate (and also: wine. Did I mention that? 😜)

More details to come but here are some highlights:

-Guided nature walk to the llama farm!

-Campfire storytelling and s'mores under the stars

-Outdoor games and activities for kids and adults

-Delicious campfire meals prepared by local vendors

-A chance to bond with fellow families and create lasting memories together

-Wine!

Reservations open tomorrow at noon. See attachments with pricing and types of cabins available. Don't forget to sign up before the best cabins are gone and you end up in a yurt. 😕 But don't worry if you do because . . . wine. 😊

XOXO,
Milly
Class Mom
Head of Fundraising
Head of PTA
Mother of Dragons 😊

TO: EVA MILLER
FROM: EVA MILLER
BCC: PALMS COMMUNITY
Subject: Important Message Re Admissions Decisions to Middle Schools

Dear Palms Parents,

As we continue to navigate the admissions process for private middle schools, I want to remind everyone of the importance of sensitivity and respect for each family's journey as we learn the outcome for most students at 5pm tomorrow.

In past years, conversations have circulated among our parent community speculating about which children will be admitted to which schools. While it's natural to be curious about such matters, it's important to remember that these discussions can cause discomfort or distress to families who may still be awaiting news.

As a community, it is our responsibility to uphold values of privacy, empathy, and support for one another. Please refrain from engaging in conversations that speculate on admissions outcomes. Each family's situation is unique, and we must be mindful of the emotions they may be experiencing during this time.

Let us come together to celebrate all our children's achievements, regardless of where their educational journeys may lead them. Thank you for your understanding and cooperation in fostering a compassionate and inclusive environment for our school community.

Best regards,
Eva Miller
Principal, Palms School

PART IV

The Annual Palms School Glamping Trip

TO: MILLY
FROM: MILLY
BCC: PALMS PARENTS
Subject: Reminder: Glamping Trip to El Capitan Canyon This Weekend!

Dear Parents,

We are so proud of our amazing sixth graders and their admissions to the best private middle schools in Los Angeles! We can't wait to celebrate and *relax* at El Capitan Canyon for a much-needed weekend of togetherness.

Please make sure to sign up for chores in the Google Doc that was shared earlier in the week. I know it was a busy one (for all of us!) so I'm attaching it here again. ☺

This goes without saying (but I'll say it anyway!), but it's essential that we all pitch in to make this trip enjoyable for everyone.

If you have any questions with anything related to the trip or just want to share some great news or a special skill, please don't hesitate to reach out to me directly.

Let's make this a super memorable and fun weekend!

Don't forget bug spray! And headlamps!

Oh, and . . . wine. 😜

XOXO,
Milly
Class Mom
Head of Fundraising
Head of PTA
Mother of Dragons 😈

TO: MILLY
FROM: MILLY

BCC: PALMS PARENTS

Subject: El Cap Schedule

Okay, okay, I know! I told you all I'd send less emails this year, but this one doesn't count, because I forgot to send this schedule with the last email. 🎒 🏕 👻

Anyway, here's the (loosey goosey!) schedule of events for the weekend (for real this time!):

FRIDAY:

4PM-7PM—Check in/Arrivals//Settle in

7PM—Jewish Affinity Group leads Shabbat blessing . . . Challah, y'all!

7:05PM—Buffet dinner—reminder to only take the vegan and gluten-free options if you signed up for those—please and thank you!

8PM—S'mores and Sing-Along by the bonfire—BYO guitar, instruments (no violins after all the complaints from other glampers last year—please and thank you!)

10PM—Bedtime (ish?!)—let's encourage kids to go to sleep relatively early—they have a big day on Sat!

SATURDAY:

7AM (oof, I know, right?!) - Breakfast buffet! Reminder to only drink the almond milk and dairy substitutes and eat the vegan breakfast burritos if you signed up and paid extra for them. Please and thank you!

9-9:30AM—Breakfast buffet cleanup

9:30AM—Hike to the llama farm (I hear they have baby animals we can pet—yay and . . . bring Purell 🧴!)—for those of you who have not done this hike before, it's less of a "hike" and more of a "walk." You can do it! Bring water!

12PM—Lunch buffet (and rosé all day for the parents!) begins!

2PM—Did you think this was time for a siesta? Sure is! Dads are organizing team games on the lawn so moms can hang—we deserve it!

3PM-6PM—Free time! Take a walk down to the beach, go for a swim in the (slightly questionable) pool, make a new friend, or just play backgammon or Rummikub with a Palms Pal.

6PM—Pizza Dinner buffet!

7PM—Bonfire, S'mores, charades, sing-along, etc.

SUNDAY:

7AM—Bagel Breakfast Buffet

10AM—Check out—another great El Cap weekend in the books!

XOXO,
Milly
Class Mom
Head of Fundraising
Head of PTA
Mother of Dragons 🐉

Jillian

A s Jillian drove to El Cap in Friday bumper-to-bumper traffic on the 101, her husband in the passenger seat, her daughter in the back seat watching the entire run of *Gilmore Girls* for the fourth time, her son playing some mindless game on an iPad, Jillian wondered who started the Palms School tradition of the annual glamping trip at El Cap. She knew some parents had tried to take credit over the years, while others assigned blame and cursed the unnamed individuals who instigated this expensive weekend-long community trip into the woods.

It was, of course, a trip that most of the kids loved, so if a family didn't go for whatever reason, that kid missed out on all the fun and photos and inside jokes and social media posts until the end of time, a.k.a. sixth grade, when the Palms elementary program ended. For most parents, it was a "damned if you do, damned if you don't" situation.

Thinking about all this was a much-needed distraction for Jillian, who was trying to recover from the fraught private school–application process (understatement), which was over for everyone *but her family*. While she had made sure her daughter knew that, no matter the outcome, her parents were so very proud of her, they did not, *could* not, have anticipated what had happened: her daughter didn't get in *anywhere*.

After the initial shock, Jillian had felt sadness and desperation. She was sad for her daughter, who had worked so hard, who was so kind, much kinder than Jillian, who was going to suffer because Jillian wasn't good enough at this admissions *Squid Game*. It was Jillian's fault that her daughter got wait-listed everywhere. She didn't volunteer at school enough, wasn't wealthy enough, wasn't connected enough, and now it was her daughter who was going to suffer for her shortcomings as a mother.

The pressure and the sadness and the disappointment Jillian felt were insurmountable. She wanted to strangle Eva, who she felt was also responsible for all this. When they had found out (Was it just the day before? It felt like a lifetime ago), Jillian called Eva, who immediately picked up and said, "Congrats!"

"What are you talking about? She was wait-listed . . . *everywhere*."

"I spoke with admissions earlier this week. It was a yes at Redford."

"Well, it's *not* a yes, it's a wait list . . . *everywhere*!"

"Huh. That's strange."

"*Strange?* My daughter didn't get in anywhere, Eva. Zero! We did everything you told us to do. We spent money we didn't have for a tutor so our kid *with learning differences* could take a *standardized* test that *none of the schools she was applying to was even looking at* but you insisted was necessary—"

"I don't like your tone, Jillian."

I don't like you, Eva.

Jillian didn't actually say that part, about not liking Eva. But she wanted to.

"Let me make some calls. But give me a beat. It's a bit crazy here."

Jillian heard a loud noise in the background.

"What was that?"

"Mags is just popping a bottle of Champagne. Our daughter got into all five schools she applied to, so she's pretty excited."

If Jillian could have reached through the phone and strangled Eva in that moment, really just squeezed the fucking life out of her, she would have. The anger, the betrayal, the frustration . . . It was so intense . . . intense like she had never felt before.

"Oh, actually, Jillian! I think this is the bottle you gave us at the beginning of the school year!"

Jillian's world was crashing down and they were popping Champagne, the Champagne that had traveled in and out of her refrigerator for years and was supposed to celebrate the revival of her husband's career and their financial future. It was all so much. Too much.

"Oh, wow. *Five?* Five schools? She applied to *five* schools when you advised all of us not to apply to more than three?"

"Well—"

"She should turn down the schools she's not accepting so kids like my daughter can get in off the wait list."

"Absolutely. But it's such a big decision, so I'm encouraging her to really take a beat and think on it."

"Are you? Are you encouraging her to 'take a beat'? To just, like, roll around in all those acceptances like it's a bed full of cash? You think your kid is exceptional? Your kid got in to five schools because you're the *principal.* And by getting your kid in everywhere—*five places, no less*—you fucked other kids at this school who you were supposed to be helping, kids who were just as, if not more, deserving of those spots."

"Jillian, no one else seemed to have this issue. I will help your daughter get off the wait list because that is my job, but I don't appreciate your tone. So for now, while I'm disappointed with the outcome, I feel confident she will get off a wait list, and I will work toward that with you. And now, I'm going to go celebrate with my family."

And she hung up.

Jillian had seethed, and cried, but also she'd had to keep it together for her daughter, which was easier said than done when all she could think of was ways to actually have Eva killed or, at the very least, fired. She had to be strong, she had to be optimistic, she had to be—and she loathed this word—*upbeat*! She would also have to be patient (not a strength) and listen to her daughter—her concerns, her fears, all the worries Jillian had assured her would never arise.

To add insult to injury? Jillian had reserved the yurt accommodations at El Capitan because they were the least expensive, and now they had to spend the weekend "glamping" with all these super-relieved families who were excitedly planning their elite private middle school futures from the comfort of their cushy cabins. It was as if every bad decision Jillian had ever made had been leading her to this one exact, painful, awful weekend.

It wasn't that Jillian didn't like the outdoors or camping; she did. She had been an avid camper in her youth. Every year, she would pull out her vintage red-plaid flannel button-down from L.L.Bean. If that flannel shirt could talk, it would tell all about her time at an all-girls summer camp in Maine in the eighties, her days and nights in college rocking out to Pearl Jam and Hole in the nineties (completing the grunge look with boot-cut jeans at her Ivy League school).

(Did she mention she went to an Ivy League school?)

Somehow, that L.L.Bean flannel had made it through every wardrobe purge / fad / sparking-joy reorg, and every move from each new camp bunk, back to her childhood bedroom, to her college dorm room, to her multiple single-girl apartments in LA, to her husband's bachelor pad, and finally to their family home, where it would live with her for . . . as long as they could afford to pay the mortgage and property taxes—which at this point, didn't seem much longer.

It had been her father's shirt, but it had shrunk so much over the decades of wearing and washing that it could be his napkin now. Her favorite part? It still had her name tag from summer camp sewn into it. There was something she loved about that. It felt so innocent, and reminded her of a simpler time of her life. A time when she was a total winner. At sports, at academics, at life. A time when her father handled everything like money, the house, school. The stress. Everything. As scary as he had seemed sometimes when she was a kid, she could relax because she knew he would make her life possible. She appreciated it now that she felt the pressure he must have felt then to support a family.

She had kept her maiden name that was sewn into that flannel. Why, in her thirties, should she have had to reinvent herself and her career with someone else's name?

No, thank you.

Her now husband, then fiancé, had been very understanding. He didn't care about that stuff. He just wanted to spend his life with her and understood her independence and ambition. She felt lucky to be with someone like him. Then.

Ironically, she felt lucky to be with him now. As much as the sex with Flynn had woken her up sexually, the gratefulness she felt coming back to her husband and their marriage and family after it was over—that woke her up in a different way.

This weekend, however, everything made her sad, even her beloved vintage flannel shirt, but she had to put on a brave face for her daughter, even as she sent out emails and texts to everyone she knew who went to her daughter's first-choice school, begging them to put in a good word for her daughter and their family. She hated groveling. She hated being in this position. She hated everything about this admissions process.

She was not supposed to use the word *hate*.

Well, fuck!

Jillian and other Palms families arrived at the guard gate, where they were checked in. As cars pulled into the lot, kids of all ages streamed out of their hybrid and electric SUVs and minivans before many could even roll to a stop—running to find friends like they hadn't seen them in years, when in actuality they had seen them two hours earlier at school. They sprinted to see if the mole was still there from the year before (it probably wasn't, because of the flash flooding, but Jillian was not going to be the bearer of bad news), they asked each other which cabin they got and who was in the cabin next to them (and if any of the cabins had been renovated, and if so, which families got the renovated ones?), and most importantly, the kids made it a personal challenge to see how much they could possibly charge to their parents' room at the general store, exclusively in marked-up candy.

Everyone's cars were packed to the gills and looked like they were going to be staying for a week, when, in fact, it would be only thirty-six hours. But who was counting? Jillian was. Families brought large poufs and tapestries to make their cabins look more boho chic. They packed liquor, water, snacks, bikes, scooters, helmets, camping chairs, cards, backgammon, Rummikub, chess, camping BBQ grills. And drugs. Lots of drugs. Especially Jillian, who planned on doing business there.

Once parked, Jillian went into the first cabin (El Cap's version of a "front desk") to talk to one of the two people at the guest check-in. Jillian put on her kindest, most vulnerable, most obsequious face to ask if there were any possible cabin upgrades available (for no additional charge). When the crunchy guy at the counter flatly said, "No," she asked (nicely!) for the manager. To her dismay, the manager, a woman significantly younger—and with more piercings—than the person checking them in, also gave her a firm no.

"But you didn't even check the system," Jillian said with a smile.

"Because I know we're sold out. There's nothing to check."

"But we're really not . . . *yurt people.*"

"I guess you are this weekend."

Jillian was not one to take no for an answer, but she sure as fuck had been getting a lot of them recently and it was slowly driving her crazy. She had been told she wouldn't be hearing anything about movement on the wait list until the end of the following week. It was torture.

So, it was official: Jillian's family would be sleeping in a yurt for two nights. Luckily, she had brought a case of screw-cap wine, a bottle of tequila, Ambien, Ativan, and of course . . . the meds that her daughter had cast off in the most recent trial to find one that would work for her ADHD without making her feel shaky or, worse, more anxious than she already was. It was an imperfect science at best. Jillian would sell the pills over the weekend—which still wouldn't cover the cost of the stupid yurt or the cost of the per-person food Milly had organized.

Also, Jillian had bought new UGG boots just for the weekend . . . It turned out they'd been so inexpensive because they were knockoffs from China and they reeked of noxious chemicals. She got a contact high just from trying them on. Still, they looked cute, even if they were slowly poisoning everyone within a five-mile radius.

They couldn't actually kill someone, right?

Hmm. These UGGs might be more useful than she'd thought . . .

She was kidding. Mostly.

Milly

Fine, it was true. Milly had unabashedly used her position as organizer of the weekend to get the best cabin. It was still rustic, of course, but it was recently renovated and absolutely fine for her and her kiddos. At least she wasn't stuck in a yurt, for crying out loud!

Poor Jillian in her yurt, and on three wait lists with zero acceptances. She honestly pitied her. She had heard Jillian was desperately reaching out to all the families she knew at Redford to write emails and make calls on their behalf. It was so pitiful, but Milly guessed she really didn't have a choice. Most of all, Milly was relieved not to be Jillian.

Milly, who had been planning this glamping trip for months, had packed her car with two huge coolers (a kid cooler and a separate adult cooler) stocked with waters and drinks for everyone, along with their clothes and bikes and scooters and gear. Her husband had stayed in LA because weekends were busiest at his restaurants. She didn't remember the last weekend night they had spent together, so she was used to it. And honestly, she felt parenting was easier when the dads just got out of the way.

She had assigned all the cabins. Milly did not like surprises. Which was why she was *furious* to see a huge digger and construction work in progress on the upper campground when she pulled in. Couldn't they do this another time? And why hadn't anyone told her? She parked and got out of her car in front of her cabin and spoke to one of the workers (nicely, of course), and they said they would be done by 4:00 p.m. Still . . . annoying. Milly tried to remind herself that she couldn't control everything, and to stay in the moment and enjoy this weekend she'd spent so much time and energy organizing.

Milly had put Eva and her family in the cabin next to hers. She'd really deliberated about whether she should do that and decided she'd rather be able to keep her eye on Eva and keep the other parents at a distance—especially Jillian, who was the only one still trying to get a kid into a school, and thus wanted access to Eva, who just wanted to enjoy the weekend with her family (and, hopefully, her lover, Milly). She felt very protective of Eva, even if Eva hadn't engaged personally with Milly since the night Flynn got fired. Sure, they'd been in meetings together, and they emailed and talked about the various initiatives and committees Milly was involved in, but Eva wouldn't engage personally, or intimately, with Milly.

As hard as these few weeks without Eva had been, it had given Milly some much-needed time to think. To assess. And reassess. Her life. Her marriage. Her family. Her mental load. Her needs. Her wants. Her desires. Her reality.

And here was the thing she'd realized: she was willing to give it all up. It wasn't enough anymore to flirt on text or FaceTime-fuck or even fool around furtively. She wanted to *be with* Eva. She wanted to be Eva's partner for life. And she was going to tell Eva this weekend that she would leave her husband and they could blend their families, and they would make it work. It would be rough for a little bit—complicated for a while, of course—but what isn't? They wouldn't be the first people to get divorced and remarried.

The excitement and the optimism of it made Milly want to cry. She was a lesbian! Or whatever. She didn't need to label anything. Love was love! And she loved Eva with every inch of her body and being, and she wanted everyone to know it! It was nearing the end of the school year; if one was pragmatic and a planner (which Milly was), it was as good a time as any to blow up two marriages and figure it out while the kids were off at sleepaway camp.

She had seen mom-fluencers she followed on Instagram write, You never know when the best part of your life is about to start, and she felt confident that nothing was truer for her now. Milly just hoped Eva would feel the same way.

As Eva's car pulled up, Milly came out of her cabin, her bandanna tied just so around her neck (olive green, to bring out her blue-green eyes), waving and wearing a huge welcoming smile. She wanted Eva to see her and think, *This is what I could come home to every day.*

Eva descended from the driver's seat, stretching from the long drive, and Milly wanted to run to her and jump into her arms for everyone to see.

But Eva barely looked at Milly; instead, she immediately started unpacking her trunk with her wife. Milly's heart sank. But optimism was her baseline, and she knew she needed to have patience.

"Tranquila," she said to herself.

Heather

Heather hated working from a moving car, but she refused to miss the afternoon for a "glamping" trip, and her son had insisted they leave early because he didn't want to "miss anything." No one bossed Heather around . . . but if anyone could or did come close to bossing her around, it was her ten-year-old son, whom she adored. Her husband drove, and she used her cell's hot spot to work on her computer the entire way up. It made her a little nauseous to work from the car, but not being able to bill those hours would have made her feel even worse.

Heather loathed these "glamping" weekends, when they all shelled out thousands of dollars for the kids to get impetigo or pinworms or ringworm or *whatever* worm, sometimes multiple worms, and would be charged for hundreds of dollars' worth of candy at the general store.

Heather also loathed the quaintness of El Cap, which some of the other families purported to love—maybe because the town where she had been raised was an authentic version of what El Cap was pretending to be. Like everything in Los Angeles (even though this was outside LA city limits, of course), El Cap was nothing more than a facade.

The outdoors wasn't foreign or scary or exciting to her, as it was to some other Palms moms, but she had moved out of the sticks in Idaho and into the city for a reason. She preferred it. She had the opposite of claustrophobia. She felt open spaces were overrated.

Also, she couldn't stand eating multiple meals with the same people. Small talk was the bane of her existence, and she hated watching people eat and talk; something about it made her sick to her stomach, and she was not someone with a weak constitution, generally. Although it was always fascinating to see how some parents used the weekend as an excuse to overserve themselves, to see which parents couldn't handle their alcohol and which were dumb enough to experiment with drugs on a family glamping trip, when their impressionable children might see them.

The worst part was having to be around Dawn and her husband, and their son. The likeness between her son and theirs was only getting more obvious as the boys grew older. Heather now worried daily that someone would put it together, but everyone was so self-involved and self-important, no one had so far. And now Flynn was out of the school, so she didn't have a teacher around confusing the two boys and insisting they were related. She felt solace in that.

And thank God she'd foiled Dawn's attempt to get into the tennis club. She had looked into Dawn's appeal, but Heather wasn't worried. An appeal would need twenty signatures, and even with Milly's help (why would Milly help her?), Dawn's husband was a notorious asshole and no one at the club wanted that element there.

Once Heather and her family arrived at El Cap, her son came with her to check in. As she walked up to the registration desk, she ran right into Dawn and her husband and their son, who were also waiting to check in.

Jillian was just leaving. "See you out there!" she said. "We'll be the ones in the yurt. Wish us luck!"

"That's so adventurous!" said Dawn.

"That's one way to put it," Jillian said. "Want to switch?"

"Uh, no."

A yurt? Ugh. Heather wouldn't wish that on anyone—er, most people. Maybe she would wish it on Dawn and her husband. But she wouldn't wish that on Jillian, who had enough to deal with right now. Jillian had become the private school cautionary tale about what happens when you get on Eva's bad side. Jillian was one of the few moms Heather could stand, so she felt bad for her.

"Oh, and a reminder not to leave any food out!" the glamping manager called out. "We have a couple of bears in the area—and remember, they're the ones who live here, not you. So please be mindful."

"But we don't have to worry, right? They're not dangerous, are they?" asked Dawn, leaning over the counter as if the answer to her question were somewhere on their desk.

"Nah. But, I mean, be cautious. And be alert. And don't leave food out, obviously. Always put the lids back on garbage cans. Commonsense stuff. The bears themselves are pretty used to visitors by now. The only time they can be dangerous is if you mess with a mama bear's cub. There's a reason they call some women *mama bears*—those mothers who would do anything, y'know, sometimes crazy things—violent and irrational and whatnot—to protect their young. I probably don't have to tell you city mamas about that."

Dawn and Heather stared straight ahead, avoiding eye contact. Dawn's husband gritted his teeth. Heather knew this look of his—she remembered it well from when they'd worked together and someone would fuck up something simple and he would want to yell or throw something but knew HR would come for him if he did. The man was always on the brink of explosion.

This was Heather's nightmare: being in a small space with the man she'd had an affair with, who also happened to be the secret biological father of her son; along with his wife; and their son and her son, who were (unknowingly) half brothers; and a particularly loquacious and annoyingly jovial glampground employee.

"So that's two adults and two kids? Twins, huh? Got your hands full?"

Dawn's husband squinted and tilted his head. Dawn jumped in.

"Just one. That's our son," she said, pulling their son over and putting her arm around his shoulders possessively.

"They're not related," Heather chimed in.

Heather held her breath. Was this the moment she had been fearing since the day she'd gotten the positive pregnancy test? If anyone found out, and the biological paternity of her son was exposed, it would upend her marriage, her life, her son's life . . . The collateral damage was too intense to think about. Not to mention, it would become a hot topic of Palms School–mom gossip, and Heather loathed gossip, especially when she was the subject of it.

And how would her husband react? It would break his heart. And Heather, as frustrated as she could be with him at times, didn't want to break his heart. She loved him. She loved their family. She just had to get Dawn and her family out of this school community and away from Heather's. At least Dawn wasn't joining the tennis club. At least she had one safe space left.

"Really? Are they, like, cousins or something?"

What was wrong with this guy? Why was he not dropping it?

"They look like twins! Hey, Pedro, come look at this—" He motioned to a guy who was outside removing the trash from a bin and putting in a fresh compostable garbage bag. He must have thought that Pedro didn't understand him, and so he broke out his Spanglish and also increased his volume. He pointed at the boys while yelling, "¡Pedro! ¡Ve! Hermanos, ¿sí?"

Heather clenched her teeth. She felt trapped. She hated feeling trapped. It was, quite frankly, why she had become a lawyer.

From outside, Pedro shrugged and went back to the garbage.

"Can we just have our key?" Dawn's husband asked.

"City people are so impatient," the employee said, shaking his head.

Heather watched as Dawn's husband looked at his own son and then at Heather's, then back to his.

Heather was pretty sure of one thing in that moment . . .

He knew.

And she couldn't—wouldn't—have that.

Jillian

W hat is the difference between a tent and a yurt?"
    Asked no one who really cared about the answer ever.

The yurt was basically a tent, but it wasn't collapsible or movable. It definitely did not have a bathroom "en suite" or anywhere close by or private, which was . . . unfortunate. Also, it did not have heat. But it did have *cots* instead of just a dusty floor to sleep on, so there was that? There was really nothing "glam" about the yurt. At all.

Meanwhile, Jillian's kids thought it was "cool" and wanted to sleep out in other kids' cabins anyway. Jillian hoped that at least one of them would sleep in the yurt with them so her husband wouldn't get any ideas about having sex. While they'd been having much more sex recently, which was good for them, she really didn't want to writhe around in an old, creaky cot in a dirty yurt. She had done enough slumming around by being at Flynn's un-air-conditioned studio apartment with the stained futon in Echo Park adjacent or wherever the fuck that was. It gave her the willies just thinking about it . . . also the sex they'd had there, but that was another kind of *willies* altogether, and she had to shake that off too. Because . . . that was over. And she had moved on.

Flynn had tried to contact her several times over the last few weeks, which worried her. She had blocked him on her phone, so he had tried to friend her on Instagram and even to contact her through her old

Facebook account, which she rarely checked. He made her a video on TikTok, which she erased immediately. He Snapchatted her. She had to give him credit for his tenacity. She'd even thought she saw him outside the carpool line at school a few times, but she knew she was just being paranoid. She hadn't heard anything for the last week . . . which, in a weird way, was disappointing but was mostly a relief. Her life was complicated enough as it was without having to deal with a Gen Z paramour who had the impulse control of a six-year-old.

The drive up the dirt road had taken them through several circles of hell—circles of *cabins*, that is. Jillian noticed a few cabins being renovated along the way. Over the years, they had stayed in some of these campgrounds, but this year, they were at the top circle, which was new for the Palms community.

Also new? There was active construction. Which took away from the "peaceful" promise of the weekend. When they had gotten out of the car, Milly had been complaining to anyone who would listen that no one had shared this information about the construction with her when she booked. Of course, there was no one really to complain to—a constant reminder that no one was putting the *glam* in *glamping*.

It was finally 5:00 p.m. by the time most families arrived, though some working parents were arriving after dinner (the lawyers and doctors—the ones with real jobs, not the entertainment people, obviously, who were "always working" but could also somehow go to yoga at 11:00 a.m. on a Tuesday).

Jillian opened her screw-cap bottle of cheap-and-cheerful sauv blanc and did a healthy pour into her Yeti travel coffee mug with a bunch of ice she'd taken from one of Milly's coolers. She took a long sip and sat down in her "camping chair."

She tried to inhale and exhale and relax, but ended up swallowing a large bug and getting bitten by something on her neck and swatting at it but missing the little fucker and getting angry all over again.

A bunch of kids had descended on the area, deciding to use the side of their yurt as the backboard for their game of handball, which was particularly noisy and annoying.

"Hey, that squirrel only has one eye!" someone's kid yelled.

Other kids came running to see it.

"He really does have one eye!"

They were calling him *One-Eyed Pete* and feeding him Hot Takis.

"That's not going to end well," Jillian yelled over to the pack of kids, of whom exactly zero were her offspring. "Did they teach you about leprosy at school?" she asked. "No? They should have!"

A few of the kids looked back at her, barely registering that she was an adult or any type of authority, and shrugged her off, insisting on getting as close to the one-eyed squirrel as possible.

"Let's get Pete to eat the Hot Takis from our hands!" said one of the kids.

"Yeah!" said another.

"Don't complain when you get leprosy!" she added.

"What's leprosy?" one kid asked another. They both shrugged and turned back to the feral squirrel. "Whose mom is that, anyway?"

Jillian took a swig of her wine on the rocks in her travel mug as her husband sat in the chair next to her. Jillian bug-sprayed her arms and ankles. She passed the spray to her husband, who then used it.

"How do you think the squirrel got one eye?" Jillian asked him as he sipped his tequila and soda in a recyclable paper cup.

"Pete?"

"You heard about the name already?"

"Heard about it? I named him."

Jillian smiled. Of course he had. He could be charming and adorably quirky. If only he had a job.

"And I don't know how he lost an eye, but I bet if you asked Pete, he would say, 'You should see the other guy.'"

Jillian smiled and laughed. She still wore sunglasses even though she no longer needed them. Her eyes were puffy from a week of not sleeping, secret crying (so her daughter wouldn't see), and stress. She leaned her head back.

"I like the yurt!" her husband said optimistically.

"You are very easy to please."

"Well, I just like being with you."

He reached over and took her hand.

"I love you," he said.

"Love you," she said.

She felt so much guilt. And so much sadness. But she also felt love. And hope. For her husband. For their marriage. For their future.

It was moments like this when she was reminded that, for all his faults, for all her disappointments in his career trajectory, she didn't deserve the amount of love he felt for her when she'd been so cruel. And such a fuckup. As a wife, as a mom—everything.

He leaned toward her, and they kissed on the lips.

Jillian thought about her disastrous week—admissions decisions (or lack thereof) and having to block Flynn on every social media platform imaginable. The same things that had appealed to her about him at first—his recklessness, his zero fucks given, the danger of them being found out, the audacity of it all—were what repulsed and terrified her now. But he was on her mind, which annoyed her because . . .

She swore she kept seeing him. She thought she saw him there, here, everywhere, even at the glampground! Of course she would look closer and it wouldn't be him. She worried that, with all the stress with admissions and their finances, she was really losing it, like, finally having that mental break she'd always known she was destined to have at some point.

Her solution in the moment? A refill. That seemed the best option. She filled up her travel mug with more wine, and as she got up to find more ice from the cooler, her husband grabbed her hand and said, "Be careful, okay? Don't drink too much."

She hated when he treated her like a child. Even if she sometimes behaved like one.

"I'm just getting ice. It's hydrating!" She gave him a wink and a smile.

"I've heard that before."

"Don't worry. I got this," she said as she turned the corner behind a cabin to where the cooler with the ice could be found. She opened it and looked for a scoop, knowing that someone as anal as Milly would not have wanted people putting their dirty glamping hands into the ice, but before she could find it, she heard a familiar voice:

"Of all the glampgrounds in all of the world, you came into mine."

Jillian knew the voice. And the dumb recycled line. She froze. It couldn't be. He wouldn't be . . . *couldn't* be. He didn't even have a car . . . and he was not *that* nuts. Or did she have him all wrong?

She slowly turned to see . . .

Flynn. Just that nuts. In cargo shorts, long black socks pulled over his calves, and a T-shirt. He carried a bouquet of local wildflowers. It was a sweet gesture, but if she was being honest, the bouquet was pretty anemic.

He held the flowers out to her. She jumped back as if she were Pete the One-Eyed Squirrel and he were a kid pushing Hot Takis in her face.

She didn't know how to process or emotionally digest the fact that her daughter's former teacher, whom Jillian had fucked every which way to Sunday (actually not Sundays, because her son usually had a soccer game, and also Sundays were for family and such), had followed her more than a hundred miles to an event in which most of the school would be convening.

She realized, as he smirked at her, that she hadn't yet spoken. What would she even say?

"What . . . the actual fuck, Flynn?" she managed to utter.

That was a start.

"What was I supposed to do? You don't answer my calls, you don't text me back—"

"Because it's over . . . between us . . . I don't know how to be more clear about that. And you don't work at the school anymore. You should not be here! Or anywhere near where I am!"

"Well, I'm here," he said.

He looked like an overgrown kid in that moment, and she was so disgusted with herself for ever being into him and allowing this thing to happen between them.

She had to defuse him, to defuse this situation before he tore it all down, everything she had built. Could it all be torn down so easily? She felt, in that moment, that it could be, and she felt genuine fear. No matter how much she complained about the state of her life, she didn't want to lose it all.

"How did you even get here?"

"I rode my bike."

"To Santa Barbara?"

"Yeah. I left on Wednesday. I crashed at a friend's along the way, got a flat tire and got it fixed—"

"That was meant more rhetorically—"

"I heard about your daughter. About admissions."

"What? How?"

"They never changed my Google Classroom log-in. I was curious."

"That . . . was nice of you. I think."

"I'm so sorry."

Against her better judgment, Jillian dropped her guard a bit.

"Yeah. Well, it's been a fucking nightmare."

"Are you okay?"

She stared at him long and hard. And then she laughed out loud. Not because any of this was remotely funny, but because she realized that throughout all of it, this entire harrowing and horrible Promethean admissions process, no one had asked Jillian herself if she was okay.

Jillian was *not* okay.

So she didn't know what to say to Flynn or how to respond, because she'd been repressing every feeling: anxiety, depression, anger, frustration, embarrassment. She had to be strong for everyone else, and finally someone—this annoying, young, sweet, fucks-like-a-champ, Ed Sheeran–loving guy—was asking if she was okay.

But she couldn't even process or verbalize any of it because she started crying and sweating. Why was it so fucking hot in March? *Screw you, climate change. Go fuck yourself, Santa Ana winds!*

She wiped her nose with her vintage flannel shirt and took it off to tie around her waist.

"I can help you—"

"No, you can't. No one can. Except Eva. And she's too busy sifting through her daughter's own acceptances to help mine get off a single wait list."

"I have something that could help. I've been trying to tell you."

"Flynn, there's nothing for you to do—"

"Jillian, I have something on Eva."

"What do you mean?"

"Something that could ruin her career and her marriage . . . something she wouldn't want to get out. Trust me."

She took a beat, studying his eager face. She sipped her cold white wine out of her travel mug. The ice clinked as she did. He reached his hand out, his eyes trained on hers, taking the mug from her hand and drinking it. He licked his lips and she got lost for a moment just staring at them. But she had to snap out of it.

"Meet me behind the Long House in ten minutes," she said.

"Okay."

"Okay."

"Just one thing: What's the Long House?"

"It's literally a long house—a cabin that's longer than the others. You can't miss it; it's over there, see? We can talk behind it. But don't let anyone see you!"

"I have a hat," he said cheerfully, as if this bucket hat that said EL CAP with the tags still hanging off it were some kind of Mossad-level disguise.

"Did you steal that hat?" Jillian asked.

"Nah."

"Okay, good."

"I did charge it to Eva's room, though."

He walked away backward, winking and staring at her with his tongue out and that shit-eating grin of his.

Jillian didn't know whether to laugh or cry. She walked back to her yurt.

"I'm going out for a walk," she called to her husband.

"Maybe I'll come with you," he said, looking up at her.

"No, that's okay. I kind of need some time to myself."

He nodded and shrugged and went back to scrolling through Instagram on his phone.

She sometimes wondered if he knew something was going on with her. If he did know, he wasn't showing it, and either way, she felt confident that he would wait for her. He would wait for her to go through whatever it was she was going through, and she was reminded, in that moment, that she loved him and that she had failed him, as she had failed her daughter through this admissions process. She felt a pang of guilt. More than a pang. It washed over every inch of her like a wave keeping her down until she gave up and accepted her fate.

She put her arm around his shoulders.

"Can we go for a walk later? Together, I mean?" she asked.

"Sure."

"I just . . . I need to check out a bit."

"I get it. You don't have to apologize to me."

But she did. Oh, how she did.

She kissed him on the forehead like she was taking a child's temperature with her lips. He reached around and pulled her into him, awkwardly leaning his head into her chest.

"Love you," he said, already moving back to his Instagram feed.

"Love you," she said.

And she left their family yurt to meet her Gen Z ex-lover—a sentence she never thought she'd think.

When she got to the Long House, she was careful to make sure no one saw her going around to the back of it. There wasn't much behind the Long House aside from more woods and a dumpster. It was right by the active construction, which had stopped, but the digger and some of the construction tools had been carelessly left behind. Jillian eyed a large mallet-like tool, registering it was there and shaking off the thought that if push came to shove with Flynn . . . would she use it? But that was ridiculous. Jillian was not a violent person. She wasn't capable of murder. Unless it was self-defense, of course. She had to get the notion out of her head.

Flynn was already there, sitting on a tree stump. He was playing what Jillian had to assume was an Ed Sheeran song on his ukulele.

"You biked from Los Angeles with your ukulele?"

"I really wanted to play you a song."

"That's really sweet, Flynn, but—"

"I told you I'm here to help."

"A song isn't going to help me."

Flynn reached into his pocket and pulled out his phone.

He held it up, and Jillian leaned in closer. She was curious what was so important, so helpful, that he'd had to bike to Santa Barbara to show her.

He pressed play.

What Jillian saw at first was dark and grainy video . . . of the floor . . . and it looked like . . . a kitchen?

"I can barely see it, Flynn. I don't have my readers—"

"Keep watching," he said.

A kitchen floor, linoleum, a counter . . . She squinted. Oh, wait, she knew that kitchen . . . It was the school kitchen . . . yes, the Palms School kitchen.

"Why am I looking at the school kitchen?"

"Wait for it . . ."

Jillian went back to the video, squinting more, as if that would brighten it. The camera panned across the kitchen, landing on: Eva. She was sitting on the counter . . . it was dark . . . What was she doing? It was hard to make it out.

"So, Eva's in the kitchen at school? I can't see—"

"Shhh," he said.

Jillian turned back to the video. Eva seemed to be writhing around . . . She wasn't just sitting in the school kitchen, she was doing something else . . . Could it be that she was . . . having an orgasm?

Gross.

But what shocked Jillian the most was when *Milly emerged from between Eva's legs.*

"No fucking way!" said Jillian, mesmerized.

With Milly's hand still firmly between Eva's legs, the women kissed passionately as Eva orgasmed again . . .

And on the nut-free counter, no less! Jillian was so genuinely shocked and dumbfounded by the whole thing that her first incredulous reaction was: "I . . . I didn't even think they had Wi-Fi here."

"I know, right? Not sure how. Maybe fiber, not glitchy at all—"

"When did you . . . How did you . . ."

"It was the night I got fired. At school. A few weeks ago. I went to the kitchen to make an organic matcha after you left and I saw them there. So I filmed it."

"You sure did."

"I find I really enjoy documenting things. My mom says maybe I should be a documentarian. Anyway, I tried to tell you, but you blocked me."

"Right. I'm sorry—"

"It made me feel . . . really . . . sad."

"I'm sorry you felt sad."

"I know that you're married, and you have a family, and, like . . . you don't think I can step up and be who you need me to be for you—"

"Well, that's not quite it—"

"So I want to give you this, so you have something on Eva. And you can use it, y'know, as leverage, to get your daughter into the school she really wants."

Jillian smiled and shook her head. "That's the nicest and also the most disgusting thing anyone has ever done for me."

"You're welcome."

"So, you think I should blackmail the principal of my daughter's school to get her off a wait list to middle school?"

"Look, I don't know about you, but in tough situations, I always ask myself, 'What would my mom do?'"

"That's sweet."

"It's true."

"So, what would your mom do, Flynn? Would she use the video as blackmail to get you into school?"

"Hell yeah. And if that didn't work, well, man, oh man . . . You do not want my mom as an enemy, I'll tell you that much."

"She sounds . . . great."

"She's the best. She says hi."

Oof. Jillian closed her eyes. Her head hurt. This was really bad. All of it. Maybe this was the thing she needed to do, as sleazy, as so very wrong, as it all felt. And, oh my God, she couldn't believe that perfect Milly and perfect Eva were fucking—but of course it all made sense now because "Anything for Eva."

"Does she know? That you have this?"

"No. I was saving it for you."

"Wow. Can you send it to me? Thank you, Flynn. Really, I owe you one. I can give you some cash if you want to take the train home or—"

"I don't want your money."

"Okay. What do you want?"

"I want your love."

"Flynn—"

"I'm not going to just send the video to you and then you block me because you don't need me anymore. I want you to give me the chance to step up."

"To step up to . . . what? Look, I'll unblock you. We can be . . . friends!"

"I almost believe you."

Jillian's heart sank. Of course there was a catch.

"So, what do you suggest?" she asked, her arms now crossed over her chest.

"First of all, don't do that."

"What?"

"Get all, like, defensive and weird. Like, I want you to *want* to be with me, y'know."

"I can *want* to be with you all I want, but it doesn't change the fact that I'm married. And so, by definition, I cannot."

"By whose definition? Society's?"

"Flynn, are you going to give me the video or not?"

"Unblock me—"

"Fine—"

"In every way—"

"I'm not following."

"I think you are."

"You're saying that you will give me the video but I need to keep sleeping with you?"

"Well, I mean, I want you to *want* to keep sleeping with me, but I understand if it's slightly different in the beginning."

"You're a hot guy, Flynn . . . You're smart . . . enough . . . and . . . just, like, move on—"

"I love you. I just want to be with you."

He moved closer.

"Flynn. Come on. We can't. Not here."

"Tell me to stop and I will. I'd never do anything without consent."

He kissed her neck.

"You won't fuck me without my consent but you'll withhold a video of someone else cheating to make me fuck you?"

"I want to make love to you—"

"Oh God—" she said sarcastically, her eyes rolling.

But the *oh God* that Flynn heard must have been some kind of exclamation of ecstasy, because he slid his hand into her pants.

Jillian exhaled as her body reacted to his touch. She had already transgressed . . . so if doing it once or twice or a few more times would justify the means of getting her daughter into school, well, this was what it had to be.

He unknotted her flannel from her waist and tossed it to the side as he kissed her shoulder, moving up her neck. Could she live with herself if she did this again? She could barely live with herself as it was.

And then he was on the other side of her neck, and he was fumbling with his pants. She could do this, she told herself, and it would all be worth it. But it didn't feel the same as it had. It wasn't exhilarating, as it had been in the beginning.

It suddenly felt . . . gross. She wanted him to stop touching her. She wanted him to disappear.

Just as he was unbuttoning her jeans, they heard a rustling in the woods.

"Shhhh . . . someone's here," she said. "Shit!"

They stayed very still until they could see what was making the noise. A baby bear tentatively came out of the woods, sniffing around the closed dumpster.

"Awwwww . . . it's just a baby bear! It's so cute."

"Fuck, Flynn, if there's a baby bear, that means there's a mama bear not far behind. Let's get out of here."

"Can we do a quickie? I'm so turned on—"

"No."

Jillian pulled away from him.

"When can I see you again?" he asked.

"Send me the video."

"So that's all you want from me?"

"Right now, I just want us *not* to get mauled by a bear."

"Fine. I'll send it. In a bit. But not right now."

"I need it *now*. We only have five more days before admissions decisions are final."

The rustling got closer, and Jillian was already moving in the opposite direction, even though Flynn did not seem to share the same sense of urgency she did.

"I'll be in touch. Unblock me," he said. "I also have to find someplace to sleep tonight."

"You can't be walking around. Someone will see you. There's a cabin under construction in the lower campground. Stay there and I'll bring you food later. Just promise me you'll stay out of sight."

"Scout's honor," he said.

Jillian ran in the opposite direction, fixing her hair, her clothes, but she was mostly preoccupied with how the fuck she was going to deal with this. She didn't have any time to waste, and while she would eventually need the video, just the knowledge of its existence would be enough to put the fear of God into Eva, so she was going straight there.

Jillian was nervous as she approached Eva's cabin . . . Of course Eva and Mags got one of the nice, renovated cabins next to Milly's. It all made sense now, and Jillian wondered what Mags knew, if anything.

"Knock, knock," said Jillian at their front door, opening it and letting herself inside.

Mags looked up, saw Jillian, and rolled her eyes.

Nothing like the warm welcome of the Palms mommunity. Eva moved toward Jillian, effectively stopping her from coming farther inside.

"Jillian, please remember I'm here as a parent, not as principal. I hope and assume you are able to respect that," she said.

"Oh, absolutely I can!" said Jillian. Translation: *Go fuck yourself.* "I actually just wanted to talk to you . . . about—"

"Please," said Mags, pushing in front of Eva. "We're here as a family."

"Oh, I get that, Mags. I just had a question for Eva about the school kitchen. The nut-free area, in particular . . . I think it's been . . . compromised. The night of the mah-jongg party."

Eva looked at Jillian, and for the first time ever, Jillian saw fear in her eyes.

"I'll handle this quickly, honey," she said to Mags.

"You promised no principal business. We talked about this with Dr. Talbot."

"I know, I know. It's just this one thing. I promise."

Mags was clearly at her wit's end with her wife. Their relationship seemed strained. *Good,* Jillian thought. She hoped Eva's life was unraveling as much as hers was.

"Let's go for a little walk, shall we?" said Eva.

"We shall."

As they got farther from the cabin, Eva doubled down. "So, what exactly is this about?"

"I think you know."

"If I did, I wouldn't be asking you, would I?"

"There's a video. Of you and Milly. On the counter in the school kitchen. And you're . . . let's just say, *not* making sandwiches for the homeless."

"They're called *unhoused*."

Jillian had no patience to be talked down to. This was the moment she had been waiting for. "Do not condescend to me right now, Eva. You know what I have."

"Where is this mystery video, then?"

"It's in a safe place."

"Are you quite finished? I have to get back to my family."

"You look down on everyone, shaming us anytime we say or do anything you don't agree with. But you're no better than any of us. In fact, you're worse. You're *the* worst."

Eva shifted her weight from one dusty hiking boot to the other. "What do you want?"

"I want my daughter off the wait list and accepted into Redford Prep. And I want it to happen this weekend. And your daughter is going to turn down the four hundred acceptances she's not seriously considering so that other kids, kids like my daughter, who didn't get any acceptances, have a chance to get off the wait list. It's common-fucking-decency."

"How do I know you won't do something with the video anyway?"

"You have my word."

Eva gave her a look.

"If I do anything with it, you'll just tell the school I blackmailed you and they'll revoke her acceptance. It's a lose-lose. Neither of us want that."

Eva shook her head. Then nodded. Then clapped her hands. "Fine. I'll do my best to get it done. I'll send out the email to the head of admissions when I get back to my cabin. We'll never speak of this again, and I'll of course have to see you delete this video . . . if it even exists."

Eva turned and started walking back to her cabin.

"It didn't have to be this difficult," said Jillian. "My daughter is a good kid. She works hard. She *is* exceptional. She deserves a shot."

Eva stopped. Without turning, she said, "You think I don't know what you say about me? You think I don't know you're selling drugs to other moms? This is *my school*. And say what you want about me—and I know you do—but you should thank me."

"Thank you?!"

Eva turned to face Jillian.

"Yes, thank me because I have *allowed* you to stay in this school. And you know why? Because you're right about one thing: your daughter is a good kid."

"I will never thank you."

"Did you ever think maybe it's *you*, Jillian? That you're the problem?"

Jillian's eyes welled with tears, but she smiled as she and Eva connected.

"Every. Fucking. Day," Jillian said.

Jillian laughed to herself. She tried so hard . . . to be a good mom, a good wife, a good friend, to support her family financially and emotionally. And she was failing at all of it.

Every. Fucking. Day.

Eva stared at her. Did Jillian detect the slightest bit of empathy? It was unclear. Eva stomped away, leaving Jillian alone . . . ashamed, relieved, anxious, but also, for the first time in a long time, hopeful.

Milly

As dinner started, Milly felt satisfied that everything was going according to plan and everyone seemed to be having fun. Kids were running around blinding each other with their headlamps, moving in groups from cabin to cabin, eating dinner, roasting s'mores, and feeding an adorable one-eyed squirrel they had named Pete.

The Palms kids were the best!

The volunteer sign-ups had, for the most part, been respected, with everyone showing up for the chores they had agreed to take on in the Google Doc she had sent out during the week (even if she did have to remind people *multiple times* to sign up).

Tranquila, she said to herself.

After the s'mores, one of the dads brought out his guitar and the sing-along started. Milly *loved* sing-alongs!

Unfortunately, she sat across the fire from Eva and Mags, who held hands and wrapped themselves in a blanket together. It was too much for Milly, but she kept drinking, kept smiling, even tried to sing along and make the best of it. She could handle this. She was determined to handle this. She knew what seeing Eva happy looked like, and this wasn't it. This was Eva trying to look like she was happy, trying to convince herself and everyone else that she was in a happy marriage. And one day, not so far off, it would be Milly snuggling with Eva and they would look back at this moment and laugh. Or maybe not laugh. But they would at least look back and say *That was then and this is now*, and then Eva and Milly would be like swans who mate for life. But, like, nice swans! Swans could be so nasty.

But when Eva and Mags started harmonizing to "Cat's in the Cradle" together, that was more than Milly could handle. She made eye contact with Eva and excused herself from the group.

Milly waited in the woods behind the Long House, pacing back and forth, trying not to cry, praying that Eva would show up. She eyed a rogue hatchet and other cumbersome tools from the wretched construction that no one had told her about, and she had a weird, dark thought about using one of those tools on Mags, but that was crazy because she was not a violent person! When she heard rustling in the woods, she shined her flashlight at the sound. She thought about grabbing one of the tools. There were bears out there, after all!

"Hello?" she yelled.

No answer. Just more rustling.

If Milly were killed by a bear, would Eva write her eulogy? If so, what would she say? Would she deliver it herself? Would anyone find out they had had an affair? Would her husband's restaurants cater her celebration of life? Milly hoped they would order enough food. And have options for those who were vegan. People really ate their feelings at those types of sad affairs.

And it would be sad. Milly was a pillar of the Palms community— but then she had a darker thought: Who would her husband remarry? Who would raise her kids? Would the new mommy be a better mommy than Milly? And would the sixth-grade moms use her death as fodder for middle school–admissions essays the following fall? Like, to show how resilient their kid and their family was when this woman/mom/wife had died an untimely death—

"Can you not shine that in my face, please?"

It was Eva, squinting into Milly's flashlight.

"Sorry. I was afraid you were a bear—"

"I'm not. I'm . . . Eva."

"I'm so glad you're here. I didn't know if—" She moved toward her, but Eva held her hand out, stopping her.

"I'm not here for that. I have to tell you something, but I don't want you to freak out."

"Okay?"

"Jillian says there's a video. Of us. That night in the kitchen at school."

"What? That's not . . . Shit. Jillian's . . . pretty unhinged."

"I know."

"What are we going to do? You're not thinking . . ."

"I'm thinking a lot of things."

"Like . . . *murder*—"

"What did you say?"

"No. No. It was a . . . joke. Totally a joke. In terrible taste. I'm not . . . I've had some wine and it's been a lot. Sorry. What does she want?"

"You know what she wants: she wants her daughter in at Redford."

Milly shook her head, disgusted. "The lengths some people will go. It's pretty sad, actually. Instead of just volunteering her time and genuinely being a part of the community and doing the work a mom needs to do, she's resorting to blackmail? New personal low. Really. It boggles the mind."

"Right?"

"Can you do that? Can you get her off the wait list?"

"Of course I can do that. I'm the head of the school."

"You are." Milly cautiously moved toward her, turned on.

"And if that doesn't work, we'll kill her."

Milly, horrified, looked at Eva.

"Milly, I'm kidding. I'm handling it. Without momicide."

Milly giggled. "You know I love it when you combine words."

"I know."

"How have you been?" Milly asked. "Aside from being blackmailed?"

"Busy. It's been a crazy few weeks."

"Yes, me too. I've missed you."

"Me too."

"And it's hard to see you and Mags together."

"She's my wife, Milly."

"I know she's your wife!" Milly shot back.

Eva looked at her.

"I'm just saying you don't have to remind me," she qualified.

"Come here," Eva said.

Milly's eyes widened. She didn't need to be asked twice. She moved toward Eva, throwing her arms around her, burrowing her head into her neck and shoulder.

"It's going to be okay," said Eva.

"We could do it, you know," Milly said quietly.

"Do what?"

"We could leave them—my husband, your wife—"

"No, Milly, no . . . That's not who we are—"

"It could be! Why not? We wouldn't be the first people to do it. People change, people move on, people get divorced and remarried. They blend families. I love you, Eva. I've never loved someone the way I love you."

"Oh, Milly."

And before either of them had processed it or could think twice or stop themselves, they were on the ground, in the grass, Eva lying on top of a red flannel shirt that lay there in the leaves. Milly moved down Eva's body, kissing and licking every inch, determined to make Eva feel so good she wouldn't be able to say no to her ever again.

Heather

Once Eva and Mags started harmonizing to "Cat's in the Cradle," that was Heather's cue that she was done with the campfire. Her husband was smoking pot with some of the other dads at another firepit. So she decided to go back to her cabin and return work emails. The glampground had surprisingly great internet.

When Heather got to the door of her cabin, Dawn's husband appeared from the shadows, where he'd been lurking, not unlike a stalker.

"I need to talk to you," he said.

"I don't think that's a good idea," she said, trying not to seem as uncomfortable as she felt.

"Is he mine? Your son?"

Heather laughed. "My son? Yours? No! That's ridiculous."

"He looks exactly like my son . . . I mean, my son with Dawn . . . And he's the spitting image of me at that age. I can't believe I didn't see it before. He's my son, isn't he? Tell me—"

"He's not—"

"And you knew all along. That he was mine. And that's why you got me fired and blew up my life? And why you're blackballing us from the tennis club? So I wouldn't figure it out?"

"I think maybe you've had a little too much tequila—"

He grabbed her wrist, hard.

"Say it," he growled.

"Don't touch me," she growled back, trying to pull her arm toward her, though he held on to it tight. He leaned his face in closer to hers.

"I will fucking kill you. I will burn it all down. Your whole world. Like you tried to do to mine. But I will succeed where you failed. I will take away everything you know and love and care about. You will not win."

As a lawyer, Heather had to deal with aggressive men (and women) all the time. But this . . . this was something different . . . This was a threat that terrified her. For all the terror she felt, she tried to keep a stone face.

"Sleep it off, asshole. Now leave, before I scream and you get canceled again—for good this time," she said with as much courage and confidence as she could muster. He threw her hand back at her and stormed away.

She went into her cabin and closed the door, locking it behind her. She was shaking. She sat on the bed and googled: *How to murder someone in the woods and make it look like an accident.*

10 Ways To Cover Up A Murder

top-criminal-justice-schools.net

https://www.top-criminal-justice-schools.net › murder

The best time to commit a crime is in the very early hours of the day when most people are asleep. **Look like** you are not out of place on the street. Tools. 7.

Missing: woods | Show results with: woods

Make It Look Like an Accident
TV Tropes
https://tvtropes.org › Tropes

> A more elaborate military **murder**, with the same intent, is the Uriah Gambit. Similar to the inverted form of **Murder** by Mistake, in which a **murder** is dressed up . . .

Accidental Murder
TV Tropes
https://tvtropes.org › Tropes

> For a killing to be considered **murder**, it requires that the death be intended by the killer or the result of deliberately inflicted injuries the killer could . . .

10 Ways to Murder Your Lover
Sue Coletta
https://www.suecoletta.com › Murder Blog

> Method #10: Chainsaw . . . For a dramatic way to prove a point, a chainsaw might be the perfect way to go. Very messy. Lots of blood. You'll also need to bag the . . .

Milly

Milly had masturbated herself to sleep on Friday night, thinking of Eva and their magical tryst in the woods behind the Long House that evening. But she woke up just hours later, itching uncontrollably. She was sure it was bedbugs, which strung her out even more.

She tossed and turned, itching and crying and masturbating . . . her brain on a loop, thinking of Eva, and she decided that if Milly couldn't be with Eva, no one should. She wouldn't—couldn't—allow it. Not Mags. Not anyone.

But that was crazy! What was she going to do? Kill everyone? She felt guilty killing mosquitoes. How would she kill another human? And a fellow mother, no less? She tried to turn her brain off, but the loop continued. The itchiness worsened. The endless night wore on.

Milly had to be up at 5:00 a.m. to set up the breakfast buffet by the picnic tables in the middle of the circle of cabins (of course no one else had signed up for that job, so the responsibility fell on her), although, given that she hadn't been able to sleep, she was actually grateful for the task. She was still itching, and it was getting worse.

When Eva and Mags arrived at the breakfast buffet, Milly was heartened that over their matching pajamas (ugh), Eva was wearing the flannel shirt they had made love on the night before. Milly wondered if that was Eva's way of telling her she was thinking of her and that their sexual relationship would continue. But Milly quickly realized that the plaid flannel shirt was just to cover the short-sleeved pajamas, because Eva, like Milly, was itching uncontrollably.

It didn't take a rocket scientist to put it together. In fact, it was in the breakfast buffet line, as Eva made her coffee with organic oat milk and Stevia, that Mags saw Eva and Milly next to each other with their matching poison oak rashes, and any suspicions she previously had were immediately confirmed. Milly tried to avoid Mags's gaze, but she couldn't.

"You fucking bitch," whispered Mags to Milly, who was cutting a bagel for someone else's kid because that kid's parents hadn't woken up yet.

Milly gripped the knife tighter in anticipation of the exchange escalating into something physical.

But before Milly would have had to extricate the knife from the blueberry bagel she was cutting to potentially defend herself, Mags left the buffet line and stormed into her cabin. Eva and Milly made eye contact.

Eva followed Mags. Milly, not wanting to draw attention to herself, kept cutting bagels and spreading cream cheese. This was her worst fear. Or maybe it was her wish come true. Or both. She didn't know. But she knew she didn't want to live a lie anymore. Why couldn't she and Eva be together? Maybe this was the opportunity? Their love and commitment realized and solidified through a shared, wretched case of poison oak?

"I'm lactose intolerant!" yelled the kid (not Milly's, someone else's—it takes a village) who was impatiently waiting for her bagel. "That's the regular cream cheese. I told you I need the dairy-free cream cheese, and now there are no more blueberry bagels!"

The kid threw herself on the ground in tears.

Milly watched, paralyzed. She agreed with Eva that this generation really needed to work on their resilience.

"I'm telling my mom!" she shrieked.

"Yes, please do wake her up," said Milly passive-aggressively.

Meanwhile, everyone could overhear the fighting coming from Eva and Mags's cabin. Parents traded looks.

And then Mags came out of the cabin with her bag and got in her car, leaving with their daughter, who apparently was the only kid who didn't love this weekend in the woods anyway.

Milly was paralyzed. Should she go to Eva? Or would that just make things worse? Should she give Eva space? Or be there for her? She was, at once, hopeful that this was the beginning of the rest of her life and also terrified that Eva would blame her and hate her for blowing up her marriage. What if, after all this, Eva didn't feel that same way about Milly?

"Oof. You have poison oak, my friend," said one of the dads smugly, a dermatologist (who, let's be honest, mostly did Botox and lasers these days).

"It's not too bad," Milly said, feeling excruciatingly itchy.

"They have calamine lotion at the store."

"Thank you," said Milly.

As the dust settled from Mags's car skidding away, Eva came out of her cabin. When her and Milly's eyes connected, Milly smiled hopefully. For a moment, one beautiful moment, Eva was hers. Milly felt so full of love that she couldn't even feel her rash anymore.

But the inscrutable expression on Eva's face turned to a hurtful glare at Milly, and Eva threw off the plaid flannel shirt, leaving it in the dirt as she turned and walked back into her cabin, slamming the door behind her as Milly tried to catch her breath.

Jillian

Jillian hadn't slept well.

First of all, she was sleeping in a fucking yurt. So there was that.

But beyond the uncomfortable accommodations, she couldn't stop thinking about—obsessing over—the ongoing situation with Flynn. She knew he was a ticking time bomb, and she had to be really smart about how she defused him, if defusing him was even possible at this point. He wasn't leaving the glampground without her. He had made that clear. She needed the video he had and she needed to keep him quiet and out of sight. The night before, she had helped him gain entry into one of the cabins under renovation by using her OXO corkscrew to cut through one of the screened windows. She had sneaked him food from the dinner buffet (careful not to take the vegan or gluten-free meals, because the last thing she needed was Milly's wrath). She'd made out with him in the partially renovated cabin and avoided penetration by telling him she loved him, but that if he wanted more from her, if he really wanted to be together, he'd have to stay out of sight for now and she had to get back to the group before they came looking for her.

She just had to get through this weekend and get her daughter off the wait list for Redford. She did not trust Eva at her word. She needed that video in her own possession as an insurance policy. The plan she had concocted was this: She had enough Ambien to keep Flynn sedated until after they had all left the next morning. He would never know what hit him, she'd have the video, her daughter would get into school, and eventually everything would be fine and he'd forget about her.

It was a flawless plan!

What could possibly go wrong?

She tried to furtively grab an extra breakfast burrito from the buffet, but Milly was watching everyone like a hawk, so she took only one. On Jillian's way back to her yurt, she saw her beloved flannel . . . on the ground! How had it gotten there? She picked it up and took it with her. Back in her yurt, she opened the burrito . . . She had already crushed two 10mg Ambien tablets with the edge of her travel backgammon set. She stuffed the Ambien dust into the mashed pinto beans and congealed cheese. She rewrapped it and was leaving the yurt when she ran into her husband.

"Oh, hey! I was looking for you."

"Hi! I was just running out but—"

"Milly said you got me a burrito. Thank you, honey. Also, she won't let me take another because she says that's all we've been allotted."

"Oh. Um . . . this one was for me."

"But you don't eat breakfast."

"I meant . . . I got this for you but then, um, Pete got to it . . ."

"Oh."

Jillian felt awful lying to her husband. Again. This was all her fault. Maybe she deserved to be found out and have her life upended?

"Okay. There are so many left, I'm sure Milly will let me take another. If not, I'll just go to the store. You want anything?"

"Nah, I'm good. I'm just going to take a quick walk."

"With the tainted leprosy burrito?"

"I'm going to throw it out."

"Okay. Walk later?"

"Yesss!"

Jillian kissed her husband and took the breakfast burrito with her to the lower campground.

Once she got there, she knocked on the window of the renovated cabin. Flynn appeared on the other side of the window.

"Good morning, sunshine," he said with the energy of someone in their twenties who doesn't have young children. "You look hot."

Jillian looked down at her stained sweats. It was still nice to be seen through his lens, as bizarre and stalkery as it was.

"Wanna come in for a little—"

"I'm on cleanup committee for the breakfast buffet."

"Facts."

"I brought you a breakfast burrito—"

"Shoot, could you get me something else? I feel like breakfast burritos are kind of culinary appropriations of Mexican culture, you know?"

"Um . . . I'm going to come back and fuck you after cleanup . . . I need you to eat this so you're strong and ready for me."

"Yeah, I guess Mexican people have to eat breakfast too."

She passed him the burrito.

"Thank you. Hey, it's freezing in here. Can you get me a sweatshirt?"

Jillian looked at the flannel tied around her waist. She untied it and passed it to Fynn through the window.

"You take such good care of me," he said.

"Yeah, well. Don't lose it! It's my favorite."

"I'm not really going anywhere."

"Okay, I'll be back in a few minutes."

"Okay, honey. I love you."

"Yup. You too!"

Jillian walked in circles around the glampground for thirty minutes, narrowly avoiding the large group of Palms parents and kids headed out for the llama hike.

She doubled back and went to Flynn's cabin window.

"You ready for me?" She looked through the screen window to see Flynn curled up, using her flannel shirt as a blanket.

"I'm so tired. Do you want to cuddle or—"

"Shhhh. You go to sleep. I'll check on you later."

And within seconds, she heard him snoring.

She pulled herself up and through the window. She used her portable charger to charge Flynn's phone, which was dead. Once it powered on, she held it to his sleeping face to open the lock screen with Face ID.

As she scrolled through his photos from most recent to later, looking for the video of Eva and Milly, she was alarmed to find photos of her . . . photos she hadn't known he was taking. Photos of her in the last two weeks, hiking Runyon Canyon. Photos of her dropping off her kids at school . . . photos of her through her bedroom window?!

Okay, fine, she had blocked him and he went a little nuts. She deleted the photos and continued to look for the Eva video. But as she scrolled farther back, she found videos . . . videos she hadn't known he was taking . . . of them fucking on his futon . . . screen recordings of their FaceTime-fucks . . . It was a veritable treasure trove of secret videos he'd taken without telling her or asking for her consent. She thought she might be sick. She was in shock. She felt violated and angry . . . but also, she was furious with herself. She had done this. She had brought this on. She was a terrible judge of character! And for all Flynn's talk about "consent," he was a fucking piece of shit. She was so embarrassed. Of course he was a psychopath.

But she had to focus. This was about survival, and she had only one shot at this. She erased every trace of every photo and video of herself she could find on his phone, hoping he hadn't uploaded them anywhere else.

She found the video of Eva and Milly. She texted it to herself. She made sure she had received it, and then she deleted the text she sent to herself and the video. She went into his recently deleted folder to get rid of everything for good. She didn't want him to have any leverage on her, but she also didn't want him to have leverage on anyone else either.

She looked at him as he slept, and she wanted to stomp on his face. She was so disgusted by him, by herself, by what he had done. And the most terrifying thing was that she didn't know what he was capable of. Who knew what he was going to do with those videos if she hadn't deleted them and didn't keep sleeping with him? It terrified her.

She took her plaid flannel off him. She was about to tie it back around her waist, but she had another thought. She knelt down beside him. She folded the flannel a few times, and she placed it over his face. She put her hands on top and held it there. She waited for him to resist and shake like she'd seen happen in the movies when you suffocate someone. She was ready for it. But nothing happened. She pressed harder but realized she could feel his breath. The flannel was so worn in that he was able to breathe right through it. She took the flannel off his face and threw it back on top of him.

"Fuck you," she said.

She set her timer on her phone for six hours.

She climbed back out the window, still in shock over what she had seen, in shock over what she had tried to do, in shock over what Flynn was capable of, and realizing that he may not forget about her as quickly as she'd thought he would. But she couldn't focus on that now. Now she had six hours until Flynn woke up again.

Jillian wouldn't use the video against Eva unless she absolutely had to. She wasn't a terrible person. She was just a desperate mom doing desperate things. She knew she couldn't keep Flynn sedated forever. But in this moment, she had things relatively under control, and she told herself that everything was going to be okay.

But as Jillian got back to her yurt, she was surprised to see Eva, covered in poison oak and furious, sitting on the front step. Jillian winced at the sight.

"Feel free to do whatever the fuck you want with the stupid video. Mags knows, so you've got nothing on me."

Jillian's heart sank. Also, she was confused. It couldn't be.

"You're bluffing."

"She left. With our daughter! My marriage is probably over. Because of you. Are you happy?"

"Because of *me*? Hey, you're the one who had the affair! I wasn't the one who outed you—"

"But you would have—"

"Because you wouldn't help me otherwise!"

"That's just not true."

"It is!"

Eva stalked off, leaving Jillian, once again, at a loss.

Dawn

Dawn had slept like a baby on Friday night.

She had put her five-pronged plan out to the universe, and the universe had responded with a resounding *You go, girl!*

Milly was sponsoring their family's appeal to the tennis club and had already gotten twenty families to sign a letter on their behalf. She'd known Milly could do it—she was sure she had to promise a lot of free meals at her husband's restaurant, but Milly rose to the occasion and Dawn was proud of her for it. Maybe Milly would even become one of her life-coaching clients? She would mention it to her. Either way, their membership was as good as done. And nothing would be sweeter than telling Heather, who had tried to take everything away from them. And why had Heather done that? Because her husband was a little bit impatient once at work? Disgusting.

Dawn's life coach business was *thriving*! She now had several clients . . . none of whom were paying *yet*, but she felt confident that with the Yelp reviews she would receive imminently, she was on the road to success. She loved helping people reach their potential.

And they had started house-hunting with an eye toward moving out of her in-laws' house in Encino. She and her husband had weathered the storm together, rising out of it as stronger individuals and as a stronger couple—like a phoenix. Or phoenixes. Or whatever.

Life was good.

Which was why Dawn was peeved the night before when she had noticed that her husband seemed distracted and grumpier than usual. He was a grump on a good day, but he was her grump nonetheless . . . and she couldn't put her finger on what it was about. So she'd given him a blow job in their cabin bathroom while their son was out roasting s'mores. She knew a lot of the other moms never went down on their husbands. Or if they did, it was just for special occasions. Dawn didn't mind it. She often found that blowing her husband was faster and easier than having sex with him, and she was sure he appreciated the effort. He didn't really say it, per se, but she could feel his appreciation.

When she woke up that morning, her husband was already out for a run. Good for him. He had gotten a little paunch recently, so she was glad he was committing to physical fitness and making his health a priority. For a moment, Dawn worried maybe he was getting in shape because he was having an affair. And then she laughed at herself because he just wasn't *that guy* and that was one of the many reasons she'd married him, and stayed married to him even after his cancellation and subsequent banishment.

Also, she had the whole family on the Life360 app, so she could track everyone all the time. Where and when would he even do it?

She was surprised that he'd agreed to go on the llama hike that morning after his run. Her husband wasn't much a of a "joiner" unless it was related to work. He was, of course, a great dad and very involved in his son's sporting teams (until he got booted off the AYSO soccer field for getting in the ref's face one too many times).

Dawn was happy to have a little fun family time together, hiking to see the llamas. She *loved* llamas. And all animals. She didn't need to pet them because . . . diseases . . . and germs . . . but her son loved to touch the dirty animals—this, she'd had to make peace with back when he was a toddler and they took him to the pumpkin patch in West Hollywood and almost got run over by paparazzi trying to get photos of Nicole Richie with her kids. LA was so annoying like that sometimes.

But also exciting. In fact, she enjoyed going to dinner at any of Milly's husband's restaurants because there were always celebs there. Maybe she would be invited more often now that Milly seemed to understand that her secret was safe with her, and their friendship could grow in earnest moving forward.

Dawn thought it must be sad for Milly not to have her husband with her this weekend. But she also assumed it might be an opportunity for her and Eva to be together. How scandalous! But also, good for them! Love was love. She wanted everyone to be as happy and focused and on the path to their best life as she was. She was a great life coach.

Dawn felt absolutely giddy this morning! She didn't even mind that her son and Heather's son had run ahead together to the front of the line on the llama trail.

"Okay, let's all get in line behind the twins!" said the llama-trail leader loudly to the group. He was pointing to Heather's and Dawn's sons.

Nothing destroyed Dawn's mood more than people saying their sons looked alike. Sure, Dawn saw a resemblance, she guessed, but they were eight-year-old, brown-haired boys who were friends and spent a lot of time together . . . Like, duh?

She made a mental note to stay focused. Their life was back on track, and that was all her doing.

Dawn was *winning*. And winning was all Dawn ever wanted.

Heather

Saturday

Heather didn't usually get nervous. She was the type of woman—the type of *person*, rather—who plowed through nervous feelings (feelings of any kind, really), just moved through them and didn't look back like she was the driver in some kind of emotional hit-and-run.

But today, something about this llama hike with her son, with Dawn's husband not far behind, and Dawn and Dawn's son, with the Palms community around them, felt like a make-it-or-break-it moment, and she had to admit to herself she was actually nervous about it. Especially once the llama-hike leader called the two boys "twins."

Heather was trying not to be consumed with the idea of Dawn's husband blowing up her life and taking custody of her son. He wouldn't do it because he wanted to get to know his biological son; he would do it to get back at Heather. And who knew what psychological damage it would do to her son? She wouldn't let it happen.

Over her dead body.

Or his.

The good news was, she was halfway through this nightmare of a weekend. But this felt like it was the big event. For her, at least. Whoever would have thought that a hike to a llama farm would be the key to making or breaking the secret of her son's paternity? She wished they could move out of LA and get out of this dumb little bubble. But where would they go? Back to Idaho? No, thank you.

A tax-free state, though? Hmm. Maybe.

Heather knew how Dawn's husband functioned. He was quite simple, actually, like most men. He was a classic narcissist, so she would appeal to his ego. She would be apologetic but still strong because he knew her pretty well—at least he used to—and he'd guess something was up if she full-on groveled (which she didn't even think she was capable of doing, anyway). She would tell him he was right. She would apologize.

Men who couldn't apologize loved nothing more than a strong woman who did. It made them feel like they'd won. And that was all they really wanted. To "win." Ha. What did *winning* even mean anymore?

She would make him think she was eating shit, but actually she would be spoon-feeding it to him . . . and he'd lap it up. He had to. She would cite her postpartum trauma as a reason for her being "not in her right mind" when they fucked in San Diego, even though, of course, she would flatter him and say she would do it over again because the sex with him was that fucking good. The sex had not been that fucking good; in fact, it was barely memorable, but Heather knew how to lie. She was a lawyer, after all.

If that didn't work, she would pivot and figure out how to make him disappear forever. She had some ideas of how to do this thanks to her Google search, which was quite informative (luckily, Alice had taught her how to browse privately at the sound-bath party), but it was a real plan B and she wasn't thrilled about it as an option.

Heather was not one of the yoga-pants moms—those moms who decided that yoga pants were appropriate to wear everywhere—but she did own yoga pants (only to work out in, as God intended), and she had put them on this morning, along with her jogging-bra top and a zip-up sweatshirt, zipped just high enough that one could still see her cleavage if one was looking for it, which a dude like Dawn's husband always was, whether he meant to or not.

Heather spotted Jillian walking in circles around the lower campground. While she felt pity for Jillian, with the wait lists and the yurt, and certainly did not envy her life, she felt envy in that moment that she didn't have to go on the llama hike and confront a narcissist baby daddy.

The grass was always greener.

The llama hike was only about five minutes of gentle uphill, but still the kids complained. And complained. And complained. This generation was so fucked. Zero resilience.

When they got to the llama farm, the kids and parents were oohing and aahing over the baby goats or lambs or whatever they were. Heather didn't get close enough to see. Instead, she hung back, standing against the wooden fence, looking away from the children and over the llamas grazing on the hill to stare out onto the ocean.

Growing up in Idaho, she hadn't had a ton of experience with oceans. The first time she even saw one was when she was nine years old and her family went to Florida for spring break. The first thing she thought whenever she saw the ocean was not how beautiful or infinite it was, but that it would be her final resting place. She'd always had an interest in fire, so being cremated was something she knew she wanted for her corpse after her eventual demise: to get swallowed up by flames and then her ashes becoming part of this vast body of water, little fish feeding off her.

The ocean was where she had spread the ashes of her newborn son. One day, she would be with him again.

The idea of death (her own, her husband's, Dawn's husband's, and others') didn't bother her. She had faced death when it took her first baby, and while the experience had been devastating, she now knew how it felt to wish she were the one taken instead, so it no longer scared her. If it ever had.

She didn't believe in an afterlife, but she didn't *not* believe in an afterlife; she simply didn't think much about it either way, because how was that helpful? They were all going to die, painfully or not, slowly or quickly, aware or caught off guard. It would come for all of them. Some sooner than others.

Heather caught Dawn's husband staring at her—probably imagining how he was going to destroy her as she imagined the same for him. He was wearing shorts. In general, Heather didn't care for the look of men in shorts, but Dawn's husband was one of those guys whose upper body was significantly more substantial than his lower body—in particular, his skinny little legs—and so Heather thought he looked unsteady, like a big block of cheese precariously balanced on two bowlegged toothpicks. The shorts were surely expensive athleisure wear, but Heather felt they were unbecoming at best.

She knew what she had to do. She moved over to where he was standing. She stood next to him but didn't look at him. She looked out at the ocean as she spoke.

"I'm sorry," she said.

He clenched his teeth. Then laughed. Then looked down.

"So, he's mine?"

"Honestly? I don't know."

A lie.

"Why did you do it?"

"I had just lost a baby. You and I . . . We . . . had our thing . . . the one time . . . and my husband and I were getting back to ourselves, to us, after our loss . . ."

"I'm supposed to feel sorry for you?"

"No. I'm just telling you it wasn't on purpose. And for the work stuff . . . I didn't seek out HR. They came to me."

Also a lie.

"Bullshit."

"You know how many flags you had in your file? You threw mugs at more than one of your assistants! *And* a paralegal!"

"That was taken out of context."

How do you take throwing a mug out of context? But she had to agree with him. She knew she would have to *yes, and* him into submission.

"I know that. Hey, I was your advocate, okay? I was always on your side. Always. We were a team. What I'm saying is that I'm not the one who reported you. There were others. And if you want to blow up my life and yours by trying to see if you're the biological father of my son, then I can't stop you. Hey, I'd be happy to have another income paying for his private school."

"Fuck you. Don't threaten me."

"What about my tone or the content of what I'm saying is threatening? I'm trying to reason with you."

"Are you saying I'm being unreasonable?"

"I don't know. Are you?"

"Fuck you."

He leaned on the fence and stared out at the ocean. She looked at his profile and his aviator sunglasses, and in that moment, looking vulnerable and confused, she saw her son's face in his, and she felt something that was in the neighborhood of compassion.

Yes, what she felt for Dawn's husband in that moment was compassion adjacent. And even a tiny bit of guilt and genuine remorse, all things she was not accustomed to feeling.

She moved her hand over the fence so that her pinkie crossed over his. He looked over, and they connected for a moment.

And then his calm turned into fury, and his face reddened like a cartoon character's, and he snarled, "You don't get to win, you fucking cunt."

Heather's heart dropped as her defenses went back up. Dawn's husband stormed away, and Heather looked up to see Dawn, flanked by twenty kids who were petting the baby lamb in her arms. Dawn glared at Heather. She had clearly been watching them talk.

Heather would grab her son and they would go back to the glampground and she would figure out next steps. But her son was petting the lamb in Dawn's arms as Dawn glared at her, and llamas ran joyfully back and forth in between them.

As if in slow motion, Dawn put the baby lamb down and started to march over toward Heather, just as Dawn's husband made a beeline for his wife. Heather was sure he was about to tell her everything.

It felt like her world was ending, her everything was about to change.

Maybe she deserved it?

Dawn's husband was about to reach his wife.

Heather hated this feeling of helplessness. It felt like losing her son all over again. She thought she might faint or explode or just scream, but she couldn't will her body or her mind to do anything.

Anything, except . . .

"Hey!" Heather yelled, not knowing what else to do or say. That was all that could come out of her mouth in that moment, and even that much was surprising to her.

Dawn's husband turned to look at Heather, and as he did . . .

He was brutally tackled by a herd of llamas running from Palms School children who were chasing them with sticks.

How these children had gone from gently petting lambs to chasing the llamas with sticks was a fleeting thought, but mostly Heather was mesmerized by the grotesqueness of a dozen llamas trampling Dawn's husband's oddly proportioned athleisure-clad body.

The crunching of his bones and the high-pitched shrieks of agony from Dawn's husband, and then from all those who were watching—adults and kids—only increased the intensity of the llama stampede. And when it was finally over, and the (literal) dust settled, the llamas were calmly grazing in the pasture below while Dawn's husband lay on the ground, his broken body still swathed in designer athleisure that had stood up to the llama stampede much better than his body did. He moaned. Dawn, in shock, ran to him.

"Someone call an ambulance!" she yelled.

"I have no cell reception!" someone yelled.

"I didn't bring a phone because I was trying to be present!"

"I don't have a signal either."

The children screamed and cried, and parents tried to redirect them, as others held their phones to the sky to try to get a better signal.

Dawn's husband whimpered. Dawn held his hand.

"You're going to be fine. Everything is fine."

Dawn's husband was groaning, trying to get words out. Dawn petted his head like he was a baby sheep.

Heather was impressed with how remarkably calm Dawn was under the circumstances, at least until her husband's guts started spilling out of the gaping hole in his side.

And that was about when Dawn lost her shit and started screaming.

Heather grabbed her son's hand and the hand of Dawn's son, and whisked them away with the group.

"Daddy's going to be fine, sweetheart," Dawn called to their son through tears.

Milly and Eva, both covered in calamine lotion, ushered the group back down the trail as the sound of ambulance sirens could be heard in the distance.

As Heather climbed down the mountain with the boys, she thought about the one card she had left to play: the tennis club. She could offer to get them in, but then what? She'd have to see them all the time. It was an impossible situation, and Heather was not used to facing anything impossible. The truth was: death by llama would solve everything.

Jillian

N ews of the llama stampede traveled almost as fast as the stampede itself. Jillian was trying to get her steps in (and stay calm knowing that Flynn was still there and fast asleep . . . for now) by walking in circles around the campground when the first Palms School llama hikers came down to share the story.

"His guts were everywhere!" she overheard.

Dawn's husband was a dick, but Jillian was sorry this had happened to him. And to the llamas. They would definitely need to rebrand. Okay, fine, not a time for jokes, but this was how she dealt with stress, so sue her.

Jillian was the first to admit that the Palms mommunity never needed a reason to drink "rosé all day," but add that they were all out of their city habitat, it was a weekend, it was (almost) noon, and one of their own had just been stampeded by normally harmless animals, and the rosé started flowing like, well, rosé . . . on empty stomachs, no less.

Some moms complained that kids were "traumatized" by the llama stampede, but the kids seemed much more focused on feeding One-Eyed Pete and daring each other to see who could get closest to the feral, visually impaired squirrel.

Jillian brought a paper cup of rosé (with another 10mg of Ambien crushed into it) as well as a turkey wrap (also garnished with Ambien dust) to Flynn, who was just waking up and very confused as to why he was so tired.

"Maybe I have Lyme disease? I have a buddy who had Lyme, and it made him go nuts, like, digging up electrical lines in the ground and going off the grid because he thought he developed an allergy to energy or something. I sure hope it's not that. I like energy."

"I think it's just the mountain air. You're not used to it. Here's a turkey wrap and a glass of rosé . . . Have a bit and I'll be back in a few, 'kay?"

"Okay."

"But you have to be a good boy and eat all your food and drink your juice, okay?"

"Can we keep doing this when you come back? I like role-play, but I want to think about my character."

"We sure can."

"And do you have a charger? My phone is dead."

"What do you need your phone for?" Jillian asked, still reeling from what she'd found on his phone earlier in the day.

"I was just going to, like, check in with my mom, check my X account. I'm starting an anonymous 'Fired from the Palms' account on X, where I can pull back the curtain on Eva and the hypocrisy of the school."

"I don't know if that's such a good idea."

"Why not? I thought you of all people would love it."

"I'll see what I can do about a charger—"

A shriek from the main glampground got Jillian's attention, and she rushed out to see the commotion. What else could possibly go wrong? They already had one dad in the hospital, and a few moms were clearly wasted on rosé and it was only 3:00 p.m. Was it still Saturday? She had forgotten how impossibly long the days could feel at El Cap.

"Get the first aid kit!" someone yelled.

Jillian parsed out what had happened through shrieking children, drunk mothers, and a nice housekeeper who had seen it all happen: One-Eyed Pete, who had become increasingly comfortable with the children who had been feeding him overpriced vegan breakfast burritos and Hot Takis for the last twenty-four hours, drew blood from one child, which caused panic, especially in One-Eyed Pete himself, who then went on what some parents were referring to as a "rampage."

The term *bloodbath* was bandied about more than once.

From what Jillian could tell, there was not actually a ton of blood, and none of these kids would even need a single stitch. But they all would need to get tetanus shots (and, knowing this crowd, months of talk therapy) . . . and so off a bunch of the dads went with their kids to urgent care.

The moms who stayed (i.e., were too drunk to drive) looked out for the remaining kids because it takes a village.

When Jillian went back to Flynn's cabin, she could hear him snoring, so she knew she had at least another four to six hours before having to worry about him waking up and possibly exposing himself and their relationship.

"What are you doing over here?" Her husband appeared out of nowhere just outside Flynn's cabin.

"Oh, um, just getting a break from Squirrel-gate over there."

"We can't say you didn't warn them."

"That's the truth."

"How about we take that walk?"

"Sure," Jillian said. She took his hand, and they walked away, leaving the chaos behind.

Heather

Dinner that night was supposed to be a pizza party of sorts. The *party* aspect of it quickly devolved into anarchy when the pizza arrived and the large order did not include a gluten-free option (let alone a vegan option), but perhaps most regrettably, *all* the pies were pepperoni.

Literally, there was not a single plain pie.

It was a group-glamping disaster of epic proportions.

Heather had been in charge of ordering the pizza for that night, but with a new executive coach, she had been instructed to delegate to her underlings more. Her assistant had put in the order, and she thought to herself that this was *exactly* why she did not delegate.

Heather, still reeling from the events at the llama hike and trying to figure out her next moves, quickly ordered a bunch of pizzas from Domino's, which would supposedly deliver to the glampground, but it would take longer than their advertised thirty-minute delivery promise. And in the meantime, there was a ton of extra pepperoni pizza, so, after offering it to several other glamping groups and employees, Heather carried a tower of pies away from the group, to the large dumpster behind the Long House.

She was so pissed off and annoyed by everything. She had to put the pile of pies down on the ground so she could use both hands to lift the heavy, sticky, dirty lid off the huge dumpster. The lid fell over the other side of the dumpster with a loud whack. For the first time in her life, Heather's nerves were shot. She picked up the tower of pies from the ground and threw them inside the dumpster and out of sight. The sun was setting; it had been a day. Heather sat down on a tree stump, alone, savoring a quiet moment to think. Dawn's husband getting trampled by the llamas kept replaying in her mind—the cracking of bones, the desperate screams.

Had she willed this to happen to him? Did she even believe in that? Would he be permanently scarred? Would he remember the conversation they had had before it? Would he remember what he was going to tell his wife? Would he remember his resentment toward her and his resolve to blow up her life as she had blown up his? Was he even still alive?

Heather was not one to daydream or worry about things that hadn't happened. She was one to take action. But in this moment, for maybe the first time ever, she didn't know what action to take. She didn't want her son to know that his father wasn't his biological father, and she certainly didn't want her husband to know. It would be scandalous. And hurtful. For everyone.

Would Dawn's husband get custody of her son? Would he be entitled to it? Would he be cruel to their son to get back at her? Heather put her head in her hands, and she started to cry. She never cried. But now she cried. She cried because the pain she felt, the pain she'd ignored, the constant pain in her chest and lump in her throat was real. She had lost a child, and the experience haunted her as much as she tried to ignore and repress it. She loved her living son, and she was afraid to lose him, to lose another child, to lose her husband. To lose everything.

She had behaved badly. She had also not played this smartly and she was disappointed in herself for that. She had underestimated Dawn and her husband. And that, she knew, was her fault. This was all her fault.

"He's not dead . . . in case you were wondering."

Heather looked up to see Dawn, still in her Alo Yoga pants, her Clare V. waist pack worn cross-body with her initials embroidered in pink lettering on the tan leather. She looked remarkably well put together, given the day she had had, though there was some dried blood or guts or both on her beige Jenni Kayne sweatshirt.

"Is he okay?"

"He will be. No thanks to you."

"I didn't orchestrate the llama stampede to trample him."

"What did we ever do to you? Why do you hate him—us—so much?"

"I don't. Hate you. I mean, I don't *like* you, but I don't like most people. I'm not a . . . people person."

"But you don't ruin everyone's careers. You don't keep everyone out of the tennis club. Why him? Why us?"

Heather took this question in for a minute. She knew she had to be careful with how she responded.

"Your husband is a great lawyer. I learned a lot from him and we liked working together. But he has major anger management issues. You know that. His HR file was as thick as a ceramic Hermès cuff. It wasn't my fault he was fired. But you're right, I didn't need to keep you out of the tennis club. That was spiteful, and I'm sorry. I'll help you get back in. I'll reverse the signatures. Or something."

"You don't need to do that."

"It's the least I can do. I want to move on and put this behind us."

"Me too."

"I'm glad we can agree on that." Heather felt some relief.

"Oh, I meant I agree I want to put this behind us. But I don't need or want you to help with the tennis club. I already got twenty signatures in an appeal, so our membership is currently processing."

"Oh." Shit. Shit. Shit. There went any leverage or goodwill Heather might have had.

"Well, wonderful. That's great, then! Good for you," said Heather hopefully.

"Good for me," she said.

"Dawn, I'm sorry."

Dawn laughed.

"I'm serious," Heather continued. "I hope you'll accept my apology and that your husband makes a full recovery." She wiped her eyes and stood up, holding out her hand to Dawn. "Truce?"

"Oh, we're not done here," said Dawn.

Well, it was worth a try.

"Sit down."

Heather hated being told what to do. She didn't have a choice. She sat.

"I want you and your family out of the tennis club."

"What? Why?"

"You heard me. I want you out. Whatever it was he was so mad about when you were talking, I don't care what it is. I can make it go away. I will handle my husband. But *you* . . . you never come back to the tennis club. It's ours now. Oh, and your son leaves the Palms School."

Heather almost laughed. She hadn't known Dawn had it in her. Had she completely misread her and the entire situation?

"But . . . where will we . . . he . . . go?"

"Any school but the Palms. That's ours now too. I never want to see you or anyone in your family again."

"Dawn . . ."

"Heather . . ."

Voices floated down the path, and the women turned.

"I'm telling you, the poison oak was back here," said Milly as she appeared around the side of the Long House.

Dawn and Heather, out of instinct, hid together behind a tree as they noticed Eva and Milly, covered in calamine lotion, coming behind the Long House.

"We need to remove the poison oak so this doesn't happen to someone else," said Eva.

"You're such a responsible global citizen," Milly cooed to Eva. "Should we reenact last night?"

"And get more poison oak? No."

"I was kidding."

"This isn't funny, Milly."

"I know it's not funny. But maybe this was what was meant to be? We were meant to be together! You and me. I love you, Eva."

Milly put her hand on Eva's hip and pulled her into her. Milly leaned forward, and they started kissing . . . as Dawn and Heather peeked out from behind the tree, Dawn audibly gasping.

Eva and Milly stopped kissing and looked over toward the sound.

"Dawn? Heather? What are you doing back here?"

Heather and Dawn moved toward them sheepishly. Heather had to think fast. But her mind, for maybe the first time ever, was blank.

Jillian

Jillian had followed Milly and Eva. She needed to talk to them, together. As she reached the back of the Long House, she was surprised to see not just Eva and Milly but also Heather and Dawn.

"Oh, you're . . . all . . . here?" Jillian said.

"I just came back here to throw out the extra pizza," offered Heather.

Eva frowned. "Heather, you really should have composted that."

That was so Eva: caught having an affair with another married woman—her head of fundraising and PTA president and class mom, no less—and she was shaming other people for their waste-disposal choices.

"Let's head back to the group. We don't want anyone to feel left out," said Eva.

And then there was a rustling, and they all instinctually took cover . . .

The seconds felt like hours . . . Who was showing up now . . . and why? The women froze.

Jillian realized just how vulnerable she was. But then, they had all behaved badly. They all had a secret, or multiple secrets. Jillian certainly did not trust the other women, and she assumed they would not trust her.

So it was both a relief and also horrifying when the figure that emerged from the bushes was a hapless baby bear, minding its own business, not vegan or gluten-free or kosher in the slightest, and it was going straight for the pepperoni pizza. It trotted along, stopping briefly to lift its nose in the air to catch and follow the scent. The baby bear climbed up the dumpster and tumbled down inside.

"You didn't close the lid on the dumpster?" Dawn yelled.

Heather glared at her.

"It was heavy. And dirty."

"The guy specifically told us to cover the garbage," Dawn added. "We were literally warned!"

"It could have happened to anyone," said Milly (the peacemaker).

"Another reason to compost!" Eva couldn't help herself.

"Let's just keep our voices down and back away slowly. We don't want to scare the baby or it might alert the mama bear," said Jillian.

As the women started to back away from the baby bear happily eating pepperoni pizza in the dumpster, they heard:

"I want my mama bear!" a male voice whined from behind the women.

Jillian and the other women turned to see . . .

Flynn.

Now, Jillian knew Flynn was sleepwalking in an Ambien-induced haze; she had been drugging him for a good twenty-four hours, and his eyes were glazed over. He wore her flannel shirt like a cape.

"Is that *Flynn*?"

"What's he doing here?"

"I'm going to be the baby bear and you be the mama bear," said Flynn, moving toward Jillian.

"Flynn, stop. Wake up!"

But Flynn couldn't wake up—or he was sort of awake but wasn't really awake, and he kept walking toward the dumpster.

"He's going to get us all killed!" Dawn yelled.

"Flynn, what are you doing here?"

"I'm helping Jillian with something secret. Also, we're in love."

Jillian shook her head. The other moms looked at her incredulously.

"I mean . . . we're not. In love," she whispered, so as not to upset Flynn, should he be able to hear and process what she was saying.

Seeing their expressions, she added, "Flynn was the one who got the video of Eva and Milly fucking in the school kitchen."

Heather looked at Eva and Milly in shock.

Dawn smiled a bit. "Oh, I knew about that but didn't say anything. I'm a vault! See?"

Eva looked back and forth between Dawn and Milly. Milly looked down.

"He offered to give the video to me on the condition that I keep fucking him."

"That's vile," said Eva.

"For once, we agree," said Jillian.

"Still . . . you took him up on it," said Eva.

"You are not in any position to judge me, Eva," said Jillian.

Flynn stumbled toward the dumpster. "My mom said I should hire a lawyer and sue you for firing me without cause." He turned toward them. "Heather, you're a lawyer, right?"

"I'm an entertainment lawyer, Flynn."

"And what's up with your sons looking alike? Are you sure they're not related? I took a photo of them and did a poll on Instagram—"

"You took a photo of our sons?"

"And posted them on Instagram?"

"Yeah—they look so alike. What's the big deal? They weren't naked or anything. I just wanted to show my mom how alike they looked."

"I had plenty of cause to fire you, Flynn."

"I smell pepperoni," he said as he moved toward the dumpster.

"Don't . . ." Milly started.

But the other women shushed her.

"There's pizza in there," suggested Jillian.

The women watched as he walked over to the dumpster. It took a couple of tries, but he was young and strong, even in his Ambien-induced haze, and he scaled the side of the dumpster, climbed over, and disappeared inside. The women looked at each other desperately.

"What are we going to do?" Milly asked.

"We can't leave him here."

"Well, I'm not staying," said Heather, already turning to leave.

Flynn popped back up from inside the dumpster, just his head and shoulders showing. Through a mouthful of pepperoni pizza, he said, "Dude, there's a freaking baby bear in here!"

A rustle in the woods. The women turned toward the sound.

Mama bears themselves, these women knew who it was going to be and that they didn't stand a chance against a real mama bear if she thought her baby was being threatened.

"I love you, Jillian," said Flynn through a mouthful of pepperoni pizza. He rested his head on his forearm on the edge of the dumpster and chewed and stared, dozing off momentarily and then waking up.

Jillian looked from Flynn in the dumpster to the mama bear, who was now appearing from the woods. This mama bear smelled the pizza, smelled her baby, and smelled a predator. It didn't matter to her which human it was sitting with her baby bear in that dumpster—even if that human was Eva—because that mama bear, unlike everyone else in the Palms School mommunity, didn't need shit from her.

"Should we help him?" Dawn asked.

"It's him or us," Jillian said.

"Jillian is right," said Heather.

"I am very uncomfortable with this," Eva said.

"I won't let anything happen to you," said Milly to Eva protectively.

The mama bear moved closer to the dumpster.

The women traded looks, making a silent agreement that they were, in fact, sacrificing one (man) for the many (moms).

They huddled together as the mama bear entered the dumpster and raised herself intimidatingly on her hind legs behind Flynn, who was happily chomping away on his pizza and drifting in and out of sleep.

"So much for our white male savior," Jillian mumbled.

And before Flynn could even swallow his mouthful of pizza, the mama bear took him down with a single, strong swat of her enormous paw.

The rest of the mauling they couldn't see since it all happened inside the dumpster, but it didn't sound great. At some point, one of Flynn's knockoff Birkenstock clogs flew out of the dumpster, landing in front of the women like an offering. Jillian's beloved flannel, now blood soaked, flew up in the air, catching on a high tree limb. Pizza boxes were launched into the sky, so that at some point it looked like it was raining pepperoni pizza. The boxes lay broken on the ground, covered in tomato sauce or blood or both.

The women watched and waited helplessly in shock and horror.

Thankfully, it was over quickly. The mama and baby bear took some of their pizza to go as they climbed out of the dumpster and retreated back into the woods.

The women, still in shock, moved toward the dumpster, looking down at what lay inside.

All that was left of Flynn Hartshorn were some strewn limbs, an eyeball, a stray ear—or was that pepperoni? (it was hard to tell)—and his penis, which remained remarkably intact, given the state of the rest of him.

"Someone call an ambulance!"

"He's obviously dead."

"What if they think one of us did it?"

"Why would anyone think that?"

"It's clearly a bear attack."

"He was drugged!"

"We all saw it happen. He was mauled. By a bear."

"Jillian was having an affair with him."

"Jillian drugged him—"

"Yes, I drugged him because he had been secretly videotaping us having sex! And he was starting an X account called 'Fired from the

Palms.' He was going to ruin the reputation of the school. And your reputation, Eva."

"So now you care about my reputation, Jillian?"

"Let's all stay focused," said Heather.

Jillian nodded to Heather. She felt she had an ally in her in that desperate moment and was truly grateful for it.

"What an asshole!" said Dawn. "And he always seemed so nice, if a bit dense."

"Dawn, you started the petition to have him fired!"

"We all signed it!"

"Yes, we wanted him fired! Not mauled to death!"

"Eva fired him!"

"He took that video exposing Eva and Milly's affair."

"He was going to ruin the reputation of Eva, of the school; he was threatening all of us."

"We are all complicit. No one told him about the bear. We let it happen. Let's call a spade a spade: we sacrificed him."

"You're not allowed to say that anymore about the spade—"

"Really?"

"It was a bear attack. It's not our fault."

"Do you trust everyone here to uphold that story?"

"Did anyone think about what would happen to the mama bear?" asked Milly quietly.

They all stopped. And thought.

"Like, what they will do to that mama bear when we tell the police she brutally mauled a human?"

The women looked at each other.

"They'll euthanize her."

"They'll kill her," said Eva, clarifying lest any of them think *euthanizing* meant making the bear look younger. It was LA, after all.

"We know what *euthanize* means, Eva!"

"No, they wouldn't do that."

"They would and they will."

"And what would happen to the baby? He or she or they would be orphaned?" Milly clearly did not want to presume the baby bear was any one pronoun or gender affiliation. "That baby would be orphaned because their mother tried to protect them from a predator."

"That mama bear could be any one of us."

They all knew that was true.

"So, what do you suggest?"

"Burn the evidence."

"And start a wildfire?"

"Absolutely not!"

"It would stay contained in the dumpster."

"Are you sure?"

"I mean, I'm no expert arsonist."

"Anyone have another idea?"

The women looked at each other, none of them trusting the others.

Before they could debate further, Heather threw Flynn's mangled phone into a rogue pizza box, lit it, and threw it in the dumpster, where the remains of his body parts already lay.

Perhaps it was the multiple pies of greasy pepperoni pizza fueling it, but the fire quickly increased in size. They looked at each other.

As if on cue, the Santa Ana winds picked up, causing the fire to spread to an adjacent bush and gain momentum. The dry conditions had made it optimal fire weather. The women dispersed, leaving only the growing fire and the bloodstained flannel hanging ominously from a tree limb.

Palms parents and kids who were not at the hospital getting tetanus shots for the one-eyed squirrel rampage from earlier that day quickly packed up and left.

As the sound of fire trucks approaching got louder, the line of sensible hybrid and electric SUVs escaped the glampground and made its way to the 101 headed back to LA, passing the lone Domino's delivery guy, who carried a carful of plain, vegan, vegetable, and gluten-free pizzas, which, let's all hope, someone eventually composted.

PART V

Epilogue

There was a quote that many Palms moms posted on social media on children's birthdays and on important days like this one, Bridge Day, the annual last-day tradition at the Palms School:

The days are endless but the years fly by.

That recycled quote was probably the most truthful thing any of them had ever posted to social media.

In the Palms multipurpose auditorium, where Milly had stood to deliver her now-infamous "Anything for Eva" speech at Back to School Night months before, stood a small wooden bridge that all the students would walk over and into the next grade, or for some, into a new—private—middle school.

The bridge itself—constructed decades before not by a professional carpenter but by a Palms dad who had *played* a carpenter for several seasons on a popular network soap—was not much to look at. Parents often complained that kids got splinters if they held the side as they crossed over. Inevitably, there were tears. And tweezers. But it was part of the tradition and the fabric of the school, and so they kept it.

The Bridge Day ceremony was scaled down this year because the beleaguered Field of Dreams project, and the subsequent sound barrier the school had constructed so the neighbors would stop complaining, was not properly permitted by the city and had to be razed and turned back into a parking lot.

They had raised more than $2 million for the project. And they were back where they'd started, with nothing to show for it. Even the handprints in the cement for the kids whose parents had donated money didn't make it through the demolition.

The demolition was, of course, not shown on the school's Instagram feed. What *would* be on the school's Instagram feed were individual photos of their sixth-grade graduating class, listing all the private middle schools to which they had been accepted and where they would be headed in the fall.

As for the one poor soul who was wait-listed everywhere, our private school–admissions cautionary tale . . . guess what?

She got in! Yes, Jillian's daughter got in off the wait list to Redford Prep four hours before tuition deposits were due.

There was a saying in the private school mommunity that, much like childbirth, the admissions process was traumatizing and painful, but once it was over, you kind of forgot just how awful the experience was.

Well, Jillian felt pretty confident she would never forget and that she would have private middle school–admissions PTSD for many years to come. At least until the college-admissions process began.

She might even write a book about the trauma. But who would want to read *that*?

She and her husband were alive, well, and still married, happier than they had been for a long time. Oh, and he got a job! It wasn't a career-changing or even career-reviving job, but it was a job, and he'd have to prove himself and work his way back up, which Jillian felt, for the first time in a while, confident he could and would do. They now sat together, holding hands in the Palms multipurpose room, waiting for their daughter to walk over the "bridge" and, subsequently, the fuck out of the Palms School.

Between the El Cap fiasco and the Field of Dreams nightmare, Milly had rocked herself to sleep for weeks, listening to the classic Joni

Mitchell song about paving paradise to put up a parking lot on repeat. Turned out, it was as relevant as ever.

For Milly, in past years, Bridge Day had been sad because her work for the school for that year was complete. She would feel empty and depressed, and what with the field of nightmares, she should be positively dark. But this year, she felt hopeful . . . giddy, even.

Because this year, Milly and Eva were both in the process of separating from their spouses. It hadn't been easy or without complication and drama, and people gossiped, obviously, but other people's gossip was just noise she couldn't even hear if she could be with Eva in the open, to live the life she wanted to live. She felt like she needed to pinch herself every day she got to be with Eva.

Heather and her husband and their son were moving to Texas, where their son would go to public school like Heather had and where the tennis club was, like everything in Texas, bigger and nicer and less expensive than in Los Angeles. In Texas, they would not have to pay taxes or deal with anyone who was "woke."

While her hand had indeed been forced, Heather felt excited to start over and get away from the toxic Palms community and the fear of the true paternity of her son being exposed. She got a job at a great law firm with a clear path to partnership. She felt bad for her son, who was sad to leave his friends, but the transition would build strength and character and, of course, most importantly, resilience.

Dawn's five-pronged plan had been executed to perfection. Her husband was healed from the llama stampede (save for a slight limp, which she felt gave him character!), they were fully ensconced in the tennis club (where she had managed to find several new clients for her life-coaching company), and they were in escrow on a beautiful home in Los Angeles.

Okay, fine, it was in Van Nuys, but it was *stunning* and *huge* and had an infrared sauna and a cold plunge, and Dawn was finally doing what she was born to do and was most important to her: *winning*.

In Eva's closing speech of the Palms school year at Bridge Day, she would not mention the mysterious disappearance of beloved teacher Flynn Hartshorn. But if she had, she might have said he was a buoyant presence and had made a lasting impression on students, faculty, and parents alike in his short time at the Palms School.

Instead, she remarked that this school year had been unlike all others before it. And the only things for sure?

The path to the end of each school year was paved with good intentions, and there was no telling what the following year would hold.

ACKNOWLEDGMENTS

I want to thank Carmen Johnson for believing in this story (and me!) from the first few chapters. Carmen, from the moment we met I knew we'd be a great team, and I'm so grateful for your support, your creativity, your sense of humor, and your invaluable editing and guidance.

Ronit Wagman, thank you for being the angel on my shoulder reminding me I'm writing a book and not a screenplay or a TV episode. *Syntax!* will forever be our safe word. Thank you for getting my sense of humor—the insecure comedy writer in me appreciated every "Ha!" you wrote in the margin throughout this process.

Richard Abate, my "captain" since 2004, when we met over an anemic cheese plate in Los Angeles . . . thank you for always being open to my ideas and for your (sometimes brutal!) honesty. Our love language may be arguing, but I wouldn't have it any other way.

Monica Corcoran Harel, Rachel Cohn, Eric Garcia, Emily Fox, Erica Katz—my uber-talented writer pals, thank you for reading drafts and for the great advice, creative input, and encouragement.

To my LA coven / sister wives / doodle moms Courtney Bright, Sharra Lebov, Sheryl Rosenberg, Jen Schuur—thank you for your tireless emotional support and patience over many glasses of white wine on the rocks and countless neighborhood walks in circles.

Thank you, Sara Bloom, for fifty years of friendship, for always showing up, and, together with Becky Simkhai and Dani Dollinger, teaching me at a young age just how important female friendships are.

I want to acknowledge and thank all my girlfriends—new and "old"; you know who you are! When I was writing this novel, I was particularly grateful for the frank, funny, and deeply honest conversations with Jessica Cohen and Adel Buzali, as well as the PR and marketing guidance of dear friends and mom-bosses Amy Glickman and Terra Potts, and of course for the decades of love and support from Jenny Fritz, Amanda Schuon, Alissa Vradenburg, Judy Sachs, Marisa Pearl, and Adriana Leshko.

Tracy Underwood, I couldn't do it without you and our weekly farmers' market hauls, our Rummikub marathons, our long walks, and our girls' trips. Thank you for being my ride-or-die.

Mom and Dad, as always, thank you for everything. I love you.

Guy, love of my life, father of dragons, thank you for being you and for all you do for me, for us, and for our family. I know you know what "mental load" is.

To Gemma and Asher: thank you for making me a mom, and for your patience with me as I learn on the job. Please send me the therapy bills. ☺ I love you both with everything I am.

ABOUT THE AUTHOR

Photo © 2024 Katie Jones

Jordan Roter is a screenwriter, TV writer, producer, and author of the novels *Girl in Development* and *Camp Rules*. She lives in Los Angeles with her husband, kids, and their dog, Alfie.